Genealogy should be a relaxing and interesting hobby for a retired homicide detective. But in Jack Oliva's case, it may turn out to be fatal...

The only thing Jack's mother ever told him about her father was that he'd been killed in a bank robbery. Following her death, Jack discovers an old photograph of the grandfather he never knew and, intrigued by the mystery, he decides to dig into his family's history. The search takes him to the tiny town of Tyndall, South Dakota where his grandfather died in 1925. But as Jack begins to investigate the circumstances surrounding his grandfather's death, he gets a surprise he never anticipated. He also quickly discovers that some old scores are never fully settled and that resurrecting scandals, even those a century old, can sometimes be a very dangerous thing to do.

Praise for Tyndall

"...Retired homicide detective Jack Oliva's heartbreaking investigation of his grandfather's death...uncovers secrets that even a detective as accustomed to skullduggery as Oliva might prefer not to know..." — ***Bryan Gruley, Edgar-nominated author of the Starvation Lake and Bleak Harbor mysteries***

Previous Works

"... *South of the Deuce* sizzles like an Arizona summer...as Phoenix homicide cop Sean Richardson hunts down a sadistic killer.... James L. Thane has a masterful hand ..." — ***Owen Laukkanen, author of Deception Cove***

"Thane writes like Michael Connelly and his Phoenix is detailed." — ***Paul French, CrimeReads***

"*Crossroads* is a deep dive into the kind of deadly conflict that a vast and beautiful landscape can produce. ... An engrossing read!"— *Gerry Boyle, author of Strawman and the Jack McMorrow mysteries.*

"*Fatal Blow* is a meticulous and engrossing procedural...."— *Lou Berney, Edgar Award winning author of The Long and Faraway Gone*

"*Fatal Blow* is one of the best procedurals I've read in years. Packed with twists and turns and unexpected revelations .... Thane's finest yet!" — *Christine Carbo, Award-winning author of The Wild Inside*

"*No Place to Die* is a two-in-one treat, a convincing police procedural bolted to a nail-biter suspense novel. A good novel gives you real people in a real place, and James L. Thane delivers both..." — *Sam Reaves, Author of Mean Town Blues*

"*No Place to Die* is an auspicious beginning to what I hope will become a series. Sean and Maggie make a great crime-solving team." — *Barbara D'Amato, Author of Death of a Thousand Cuts*

"An excellent debut..." — *The Poisoned Pen Booknews*

"An engaging police procedural that hooks the audience. ... Readers will relish James L. Thane's tense thriller." — *The Mystery Gazette*

"A fast action thriller" — *Suspense Magazine*

TYNDALL

James L. Thane

Moonshine Cove Publishing, LLC
Abbeville, South Carolina U.S.A.
First Moonshine Cove Edition May 2021

ISBN: 9781952439094

Library of Congress LCCN: 2021908699

Cover images author photos; cover and interior design by Moonshine Cove staff

James L. Thane was born and raised in western Montana. He has worked as a janitor, a dry cleaner, an auto parts salesman, a sawyer, an ambulance driver, and a college professor. Always an avid reader, Thane was introduced to the world of crime fiction at a tender age by his father  and mother who were fans of Erle Stanley Gardner and Agatha Christie, respectively. He began his own writing career by contributing articles on intramural basketball games to his high school newspaper. He is the author of four novels featuring Phoenix homicide detective Sean Richardson: *No Place to Die*, *Until Death*, *Fatal Blow*, and *South of the Deuce*. He has also written a stand-alone mystery novel, *Crossroads*, which is set in the Flathead Valley of northwestern Montana. Jim is active on Goodreads, and you may also find him on Facebook, Twitter and at his website. He divides his time between Scottsdale, Arizona and Lakeside, Montana.

www.jameslthane.com

Other Works

The Sean Richardson Series

No Place to Die

Until Death

Fatal Blow

South of the Deuce

The Flathead Valley Series

Crossroads

Nonfiction

A Governor's Wife on the Mining Frontier

This book is for the grandchildren of Charles L. Bohac

1.

Once, when I was a very young boy, I asked my mother how my grandfather—her father—had died. She told me that he'd been killed in a bank robbery and then she quickly changed the subject and never mentioned his name again. Only years later, after my mother was gone, did I learn that my grandfather had been the robber.

2.

My name is Jack Oliva. Fifty-two years ago, I graduated from the University of Arizona with a degree in history that left me with a pretty sour view of the human condition. It also left me ill-equipped to make a living at much of anything that might remotely involve history, and so on something of a whim, I decided to become a cop. I joined the Phoenix P.D., and after five years as a patrolman, I became a detective in the Robbery Division. Three years after that, I graduated into Homicide and there I found my mission in life.

For twenty-seven years, I investigated murders, one after another. Some of them were genuine mysteries, with no clear suspects and very little evidence. But most of them were just plain stupid—domestic disputes, barroom brawls and the like that got out of hand, leaving somebody dead and the killer, usually drunk and dumbfounded, often still waiting at the scene when the first patrol officers arrived. In either event, I spent a career committed to the task of finding justice for the victims, for their families, and for the larger community. Sometimes I succeeded and, regrettably, sometimes I failed. But I always gave it my best shot, burning through two marriages and a series of relationships until I finally pulled the plug and retired at the age of fifty-eight.

I spent another six years working for a private security firm, making a second salary to supplement my P.D. pension while I waited to qualify for Medicare. On my sixty-fifth birthday, I retired for a second time and went back to reading history while I restored my house, a small brick bungalow in Phoenix's historic Willo District.

When my mother died three months ago, I inherited about a hundred thousand dollars after all her medical expenses had been paid. Her estate also included a small cardboard box about twenty-four inches long, fifteen inches wide and seven inches deep. I found it buried in the back of the closet in her guest bedroom, and in the box were maybe two hundred black and white photos that appeared to date from the period before my mother had married my father.

My dad had been the photographer in our family and brought into his marriage to my mother a couple of albums containing photos dating back to his birth, all of which were neatly mounted and labeled in the order that his life had unfolded. From that point on, he expanded his collection, filling several additional albums with pictures of me, my mom and the three of us together on vacations, at holidays, and simply hanging around the house. In his study, he had a framed photograph of my mother that had been taken when she was in her early twenties, but silly as it may seem, it had never occurred to me to wonder why there were no other photos of her life from the time before she met my father. Some damned detective I must have been.

I was now apparently looking at those pictures which, for some reason, my mother had elected never to organize or display. The box looked like it hadn't been opened in years, and I wondered when she might have last looked at them—or if she had ever looked at them again after consigning them to the box.

Slowly sorting through the pictures, I found scores of photos that had been apparently taken in Montana where my mother and grandmother lived for several years beginning in the middle 1930s. I found several others that my mother, or someone, had taken in California where, as a young woman, she had briefly worked before returning to Montana and marrying my father. I recognized the faces of a few aunts and uncles in their much younger days, but most of the pictures meant nothing to me.

Near the bottom of the box, I found a picture of my mother and one of her cousins as high school girls in Hamilton, Montana. That was followed by a handful of pictures of my mother and her three brothers as very young children in Tyndall, South Dakota, where my mother was born and spent her childhood.

Setting those pictures aside, I next found a badly faded postcard that had been mailed four months after my mother was born. It was postmarked in Sioux Falls, South Dakota and addressed to "Miss Marie Kratina, Tyndall, S.D." The front of the card showed an illustration of the Sioux Falls Center Fire Department, and the message on the back read, "Dear Marie, Are you a good girl or do you keep Mama up pretty much at night? With love, Papa." And just under the postcard, lying at the bottom of the box, was the first picture of my grandfather that I had ever seen.

The photo was lying face down, and written in faded cursive on the back of the picture were the words, "Charles Kratina, 1909." Below that, written in a different hand, were the words, "Your Daddy, Marie."

I slowly turned the picture over and found myself looking at a studio photo of a young man with a long oval face and wavy dark hair, parted from the right to the left. He was dressed in a dark suit and a formal white shirt with a wing collar and a wide tie, tied with a narrow knot.

The picture is scratched in several places as if the negative might have been damaged, and my grandfather is looking off to the right of the camera. It's a handsome face, totally clear and unlined, with a broad nose, medium lips, and relatively thin eyebrows. Like his grandson, he had mildly protruding ears.

At the time the picture was taken, he would have been thirty-two years old, a graduate of the Omaha Business College, and the Treasurer of Bon Homme County, South Dakota. He was also the chief of the Tyndall Volunteer Fire Department, and at that moment, he had sixteen years to live.

3.

I sat there on the floor of my mother's house for ten or fifteen minutes, staring at the photo and trying to divine something of the man captured in it, but I failed to come up with anything of consequence. I thought I noticed a mild family resemblance, but that may have just been my mind playing tricks on me. At six foot two and a hundred and seventy pounds, I'm fairly slender like the man in the photo. My eyes are light blue while his are dark. My hair is much longer than his and while it was once as dark as my grandfather's, it's lighter now that it's turning mostly gray.

After several minutes, I finally gathered the pictures back into the box and took them home with me. There, I scanned the photo of my grandfather into my computer, played around with it a bit in Photoshop, and then made a five-by-seven print. I put the print in a spare black frame that I found in a drawer and set it on my desk.

Over the next couple of weeks, my grandfather and I stared at each other across the top of the desk without really getting to know each other very well. I spent much of that time chiding myself for my prior lack of curiosity about the man and regretting the fact that I hadn't raised the issue with my mom again much later in both of our lives. But the only time I ever mentioned him to her, she'd made it very clear that she didn't want to talk about him, and even now something told me that it was not a subject I should have ever raised again, even fifty or sixty years down the road.

Why had she been so reticent to discuss him? Why was his photo buried in the bottom of a cardboard box and left for years in a closet? Why did my mother and grandmother never speak his name or remember his birthday or the anniversary of his death?

The man had been killed in a bank robbery. Based on what my mother had told me, I imagined that he had been a customer in the bank when the robbers burst in and that they had shot him during the course of the robbery. Or perhaps he had worked in the bank and hadn't cooperated quickly enough with the robber or robbers who had killed him. But where was the disgrace in that? Why would that have caused my mother and grandmother to shut him out of the rest of their lives and out of mine as well?

Or, it occurred to me, perhaps the fact that he was killed in a bank robbery was only incidental to the fact. Perhaps he had done something entirely different that had produced this reaction in my mother and grandmother. Had he cheated on my grandmother? Could he have been in the process of leaving her when he accidentally walked into a bank at exactly the wrong moment? Staring at his picture, I would have said that my grandfather didn't look to be that kind of a guy. But then who the hell ever knows?

After contemplating the picture for two weeks, I realized that I would have no peace in the matter until I had a better understanding of what might have actually happened to the man. Sadly, my mother had left behind no diary, papers or letters that might have shed any light on the mystery and so, like any good detective in the twenty-first century, I turned first to Google.

My grandfather had sent the postcard to my mother late in 1919, and I knew that my mother and grandmother had moved to Montana in the middle 1930s. Therefore, my grandfather must have been killed sometime during the 1920s or early '30s. There could not have been that many bank robberies in Tyndall, South Dakota during that period, especially ones in which people had been killed, and so I started by searching for "bank robberies Tyndall South Dakota 1920s."

That produced the usual raft of crap that you get on Google and sorting through it, I found nothing that referenced any bank robberies. I then tried Googling several variations of my grandfather's name. That produced a couple of pictures of men, apparently still alive, who shared my grandfather's name but who looked nothing like him at all. It also produced several opportunities to purchase an address and a background check on Charles Kratina, but I doubted very much that this would produce anything of value for the Charles Kratina in whom I was interested.

Following all of that, however, was the photo of a gravestone for Charles Kratina with his birth and death dates listed below his name. I clicked on the image and the link took me to a site called South Dakota Gravestones, which was apparently a site for genealogists. The site indicated that my grandfather had died on May 20, 1925 and had been buried in the Czech National Cemetery in Bon Homme County, South Dakota. I couldn't imagine that there could have been two Charles Kratinas who would have died in Tyndall at roughly the same time; surely this had to be the right man.

Now having my first solid lead, I turned to Ancestry.com. Following various links from there, I discovered that my grandfather had been born in Crete, Nebraska on April 20, 1877 to parents who had immigrated from Bohemia ten years earlier. Following him through the census reports, I learned that he had moved to Tyndall from Nebraska in 1902, most likely to join the family of his elder sister who had moved there several years earlier. He apparently met my grandmother in Tyndall, and they were married there on February 2, 1909. They would ultimately have four children, three boys and my mother who was third in line.

After serving as the Treasurer of Bon Homme County, my grandfather later became the Tyndall City Auditor. In 1917, he went to work as the Assistant Cashier of the Security Bank in Tyndall. He was still employed there at the time of his death, which cleared up the question of what he was doing in the bank at the time of the robbery. That assumed, of course, that it was the Security Bank that had been robbed and not another that my grandfather might have been visiting on that fateful day.

Armed with that information, I went to Newspapers.com, a newspaper archive linked to Ancestry.com. I entered "Charles Kratina Tyndall" into the search box, and when the screen refreshed, the world shifted on its axis. I found myself looking at a story from the *Argus-Leader* in Sioux Falls, South Dakota, and a banner headline which read, "Tyndall Banker Takes Own Life."

The story, dated May 20, 1925, went on to say that Charles Kratina, the assistant cashier of the Security Bank in Tyndall, had shot himself to death in the bank's vault that morning, after shortages had been discovered in the bank's accounts. Additional stories from the *Argus-Leader* and other regional papers indicated that the shortages amounted to about $48,000.

Two days after my grandfather's death, the *Daily Deadwood Pioneer-Times* of Deadwood, South Dakota, reported that my grandfather had left a suicide note with his signature scrawled at the bottom before shooting himself in the neck with a shotgun that belonged to the bank. The note read, "I sincerely apologize to all of those I have wronged. Please help my poor family as they will be destitute, and God bless them all for how I love them."

Following the trail of the story through various newspapers, I learned that the bank's head cashier, a man named George Benson, had initially claimed that he knew nothing about the shortages. The bank's board of directors apparently found that argument a hard sell, though, and a couple of days after my grandfather's death, Benson admitted that, in fact, he *had* known about the missing funds.

He now explained that he had discovered the shortages in April during a routine examination of the bank's cash accounts. He said that he had confronted my grandfather about the matter and that my grandfather had confessed to taking the money in a scheme that involved cashing worthless checks for an out-of-state accomplice.

According to Benson, my grandfather insisted that he only intended to "borrow" the money for a short period for an investment and promised that he would repay it within a few days. Benson said that my grandfather had begged him for an opportunity to return the funds and that Benson had agreed to the request.

"At heart," Benson was quoted as saying, "I knew that Charlie was a good man, and I did not want to see him disgraced in front of his family and the whole community. I didn't want to see him go to jail, and so I agreed to give him some time. I know what I did was wrong. I know I should have immediately reported the shortage, but Charlie was my friend, and we had worked together for a long time.

"I kept pressing him about the matter and told him that I couldn't give him much more time. He kept promising to redeem the checks within a few days, and then early in May, we learned that the state bank examiners would be coming in to do a routine audit. Apparently, Charlie couldn't get the money together before then, and we all know what happened next. I'm so very, very sorry, and I blame myself. Perhaps if I had spoken up the minute I discovered the money was missing, things would have turned out differently."

The papers then reported that, following this admission, the bank's directors had "sharply criticized" Benson for not alerting them to the problem immediately. They had not, however, fired the man. He kept his job, but in the end, it really didn't matter. Further investigation revealed that the shortages actually totaled a little over $200,000, which was too big an amount at that time for a bank that small to absorb, and two weeks after my grandfather's death, the bank failed and closed its doors.

Checking the 1930 census, I discovered that George Benson was still living in Tyndall at that time and owned a farm implement dealership. Ten years later, the census indicated that Benson still lived in Tyndall and that he still owned the farm implement dealership, and from there, the trail, at least in the census, went cold. The 1950 U.S. Census would not be made available to the public until 2022, and so there was no hope of following him any further through the census records. But then the guy was already sixty years old in 1940, and so he probably wouldn't have been appearing in that many more census reports anyhow.

4.

I decided that it was probably time to step back and get a better understanding of the broader picture. Accordingly, I spent several hours poking around on the Internet, researching the history of Tyndall and Bon Homme County. I discovered that the county was tucked into the southeast corner of the state, bordering Nebraska on the south and very close to Iowa in the east. It had been founded in 1862 and consisted of 564 square miles of gently rolling prairie, most of which were devoted to agriculture.

The county had reached its peak population in 1920 at 11,940 people. From there the population had begun the slow decline that had characterized so many of the nation's rural areas during the Twentieth century. It fell by a couple of hundred souls in the 1920s, but the Great Depression of the '30s apparently took a very heavy toll on the county, and the population dropped by over 1500, or twelve and a half percent, during that decade. The county's estimated population for 2017 was just under seven thousand.

During the 1920s, there were five very small towns in the county, including Tyndall, the county seat, which was located almost precisely in the center of the county. The 1920 census indicated that 1,405 people were living in the town, a number which would have included my grandparents and their first three children. I assumed that the community existed to serve the needs of the surrounding farmers who made up the bulk of the county's population.

By 2017, Tyndall's population had fallen to barely a thousand souls and the town was billing itself as "A place where families grow." The town's website seemed to confirm the fact that it was a very small community with a handful of businesses, most of which appeared to be located along a single main street. Clicking on the website's Business and Service Directory, I found essentially what one might have expected in such a town: a couple of restaurants and bars, four churches, a couple of feed stores, one lawyer's office, and what I thought was a surprising number of auto repair shops. There was a lumber company, a bakery, a bowling alley, a gas station/convenience mart, an antique gallery, and Leann's P. C. Repair Shop. Given that Tyndall was still the county seat, there were also several county offices housed in the town.

Under the "Banking" heading was the Security State Bank at 1600 Main Street. According to the bank's website, it had been chartered on November 1, 1932, and had moved to its current location in 1934. The photo showed a building with an impressive stone front, including several columns that looked like they might have been imported from ancient Greece or Rome. Also, on the list was "The Benson Farm Implement Company of Tyndall."

The website contained photos of several of the local establishments, including the Benson company, which appeared to be a John Deere dealership that took up the better part of a full city block at the north end of Main Street. By all appearances, it was easily the most prosperous business in the community.

I detoured to the Benson company website, which noted that the business had been established in 1928, and that it had on hand a "huge inventory" of new and used agricultural equipment. It also had a large parts and service department, and one photo showed a couple of service trucks lined up, apparently ready to race out to the fields if any customer's equipment should suddenly break down in the middle of harvest or at some other critical time. The site boasted that Benson's was "still proudly family-owned and operated," and that it was "one of the largest farm implement dealers in the Upper Midwest." It urged potential customers to "call or visit one of our company's sales representatives and make a great deal today!"

Returning to the Tyndall webpage, I clicked through a number of the other photos, and on the seventh selection I found myself looking at a picture of the Dugout. It was apparently a sports bar, and like most of the others along the main street, the brick and stone building that housed the establishment was obviously decades old. Glowing neon signs in the front windows advertised several brands of beer. A red and black sign in the window of the front door urged people to "Come on in. We're open!" And above the door, etched in stone across the front of the building, were the words "The Security Bank of Tyndall."

I suddenly understood that I was almost certainly looking at the building where my grandfather had taken his own life. The realization produced a reaction impossible to describe—shock and disbelief, but also a sudden and profound sadness for the death of a man I had never known, a man about whom I knew virtually nothing, and a man whose picture I had never even seen until a couple of weeks ago.

I spent a few minutes looking back and forth between the picture of the building on my computer screen and the photo of my grandfather that sat on my desk, trying to imagine what might have led him to first embezzle all that money from the bank and then to take his own life.

And what had become of the money?

The newspaper reports made it clear that none of the stolen funds had been recovered, and certainly my grandmother hadn't had it. As my grandfather's suicide note suggested, his actions had left his family destitute. I remember hearing that at one point, my grandmother had been forced to farm out her two oldest sons to relatives, presumably because she had been unable to care for them herself.

I knew that in the years following my grandfather's death, she had continued to live in Tyndall, and I also knew that in 1930, she had married again, this time to a widowed storekeeper with two small children of his own whom she had known since they were both teenagers. Sadly, though, this marriage lasted only a couple of years before the storekeeper died of a heart attack, leaving my grandmother widowed and alone again.

She never remarried. Shortly after the death of her second husband, she took my mother and moved west to Hamilton, Montana, following one of her brothers who had become the sheriff of Ravalli County. She worked at a cannery and as a laundress in Hamilton while my mother finished high school and grew to become a young woman. My mother would eventually meet my father at a party in Hamilton while he was on leave from the Navy, and they married a few months later when he was home again on another leave. I was born in Hamilton a little over nine months after that, while my father was still off on an aircraft carrier in the Pacific, waiting to be released from the Navy. Upon his return home, my parents and I lived briefly in Hamilton, but we then moved fifty miles north to Missoula where I lived until I graduated from Loyola High School and left for college at ASU.

A couple of years after we moved to Missoula, my grandmother came to live with us, and she remained a part of our household until she ultimately went into a nursing home two years before her death when I was a junior in high school. Like my mother, she never mentioned my grandfather, although she did return to using his last name rather than continuing to use the name of her second husband. I had no way of knowing if this was because she still had some residual affection for the man or if it was simply more convenient, given that her children all bore his name.

Ours was not a particularly warm and fuzzy relationship. As a child growing up, my grandmother maintained her distance and impressed me as a tough old bird. She was a strict disciplinarian and bore little or no resemblance to the stereotypical loving grandmother who dotes on her grandchildren, spoiling them whenever given the opportunity.

My strongest memory of the woman dated back to a time when I was five or six years old. I'd come down with a cold and was left in my grandmother's care while my parents were out to dinner with friends. I've never known whether her action was dictated by a genuine concern for my well-being or if she was simply sick and tired of my coughing and complaining. Whichever the case, she decided to "treat" my condition with a healthy shot of my father's Jim Beam. To this day, I vividly remember drinking the whiskey, and then I remember nothing at all of the next ten or twelve hours. Sad to say, I don't even remember if the treatment cured me.

During the years that my grandmother lived with us, she and I maintained something approaching a "correct" relationship, which is to say that we tolerated each other and attempted to be polite to and considerate of each other most of the time. Occasionally, though, one of us would do something that frustrated or angered the other, and we would exchange words, sometimes harshly.

Looking back, it occurs to me that I sometimes acted like a little jerk. At that time, of course, I had no conception of the truly awful hand that life had dealt my grandmother, and it now occurred to me that the poor woman had every right in the world to be bitter and difficult. Given what I'd discovered over the last few days, I felt ashamed and wished that I would have been a better and more understanding grandson. Glancing over at my grandfather's photo, I wished that I could have an opportunity to apologize to her. But then, maybe so did he.

5.

On Saturday night, I had a date with Annie, a woman I'd been seeing for the last few months. A few weeks before we met, I'd briefly returned to the Phoenix P.D. Homicide Division as a volunteer, assisting with a case that echoed back to one that I'd investigated years earlier. During the course of the investigation, I'd managed to get myself shot, something that had never happened to me in all the years I was on the job officially, and I wound up in St. Joseph's hospital.

The wound was not life-threatening, but it did keep me in the hospital for several days, and Annie was the nurse who was principally in charge of my care. She was a very attractive brunette who had recently been divorced, and even though she was a good bit younger than I, and even though I was under the influence of some fairly serious drugs at the time, there seemed to be a nice chemistry between us.

While she was in and out of the room, spending perhaps more time than was strictly essential to my care, we discovered that we had similar tastes in music. It appeared that we also had a number of other interests in common, and as she wheeled me out the door at the end of my stay, she gave me a card with her phone number.

Fortunately, I was in excellent health and had been working out regularly prior to getting shot, and so I healed fairly quickly. Once I was in condition to be out and about again, I dug out the card Annie had given me and invited her out to dinner. It was immediately clear that the attraction we'd first felt for each other was genuine, and in fairly short order we were seeing each other on a regular basis. In addition to being very attractive physically,

Annie was a strong, smart, independent woman—all qualities that appealed to me very much.

In the wake of her divorce, she was in no rush to be entangled in a relationship that would in any way restrict her independence, and for that matter, neither was I. We spent several nights a week together, which seemed about right to each of us and over time had grown to care for each other in a way that might have amounted to love. Neither of us had yet invoked the word, but we had agreed to see each other exclusively and I genuinely looked forward to the time we spent together.

When I rang her doorbell at seven o'clock, she was waiting and ready to go, wearing heels and a simple black dress that hugged her figure. A small gold necklace completed the outfit and looking at her I suddenly found myself wishing that we could just forget about dinner and fast-forward a couple of hours or so. But I gave her a quick kiss, walked her out to the car, and we got to Spiga, a restaurant in north Scottsdale, five minutes ahead of our seven-thirty reservation.

Since it was a Saturday night, the place was jammed, but the hostess was still able to offer us a choice of eating inside or out. Given that it was a beautiful evening with the temperature somewhere in the low seventies, we opted for outside and the hostess escorted us to a table for two along the railing that separated the patio from the sidewalk. Annie ordered a Sauvignon Blanc while I opted for my usual Tanqueray and Tonic, and we caught each other up on the events of the last couple of days. She was keenly interested in the research that I was doing into my grandfather's life and death and when I brought her up to date, she took a sip of wine and said, "So, what are you going to do now?"

I took a sip of my own drink and set it down on the table. "I'll continue to dig around on the Internet for a little while, but I think I've accomplished about as much as I'm going to be able to do there. I'm toying with the idea of flying up to Tyndall to see what, if anything more, I might be able to discover up there."

"What do you think you're going to find?"

I shrugged. "Nothing, I'd imagine. The whole thing seems pretty cut and dried, but now that I've got my teeth into it, I'd really just like to walk the ground a bit and see if I can't at least get some sort of feel for my grandfather and for what his family's life might have been like in Tyndall. I mean, it's so damned odd, Annie. Three weeks ago, I knew nothing about the man at all, and now I can't seem to get him out of my mind."

She nodded and I continued, "There is a local museum of some sort up there as well as a public library. I don't know what their collections might amount to, but certainly they must have some material about the town in the Twenties and perhaps about my grandfather as well that isn't available on the Internet. More than anything, though, I find that I'm haunted by that picture of the building where he died. If nothing else, I guess I'd just like to go up to the Dugout and have a drink in his honor."

6.

I spent the night at Annie's, and on Sunday morning we went out for a late brunch at Local Bistro. We then drove up to Cave Creek and spent the afternoon browsing in and out of the shops and simply enjoying the laid-back vibe of the small community, which on Sunday afternoons was always overrun with bikers and cowboys who coexisted in a peaceful harmony. I dropped Annie back at her house at little after five o'clock, and we agreed to have dinner again on Tuesday night.

Back home, I fired up my computer and logged on to the Internet. I found myself increasingly curious about George Benson, the head cashier of the Security Bank who had been censured for not immediately reporting my grandfather's embezzlement. Obviously, he had lost his job when the bank failed, but, if one could believe the census reports, he still seemed to have come out all right in the end.

I signed on to Newspapers.com and plugged his name and the word "Tyndall" into a dialog box. The search produced a handful of hits, most of which were related to his position at the bank and the crisis that had led to the bank's demise. I also found an obituary in a Sioux Falls newspaper, indicating that Benson had died on September 1, 1947, after a brief battle with cancer. He'd left behind a widow, Ellen, and four children, ranging in age from forty-one down to thirty-three.

The obituary noted that Benson had been born in Deadwood, South Dakota in 1880, and that he had moved to Tyndall in 1915 to take the job as head cashier at the Security Bank. The obit offered no details of Benson's life prior to arriving in Tyndall, save for the fact that he had married his wife, Ellen, in June of

1905. As I already knew, Benson had founded the farm implement dealership in 1928, and the obituary indicated that he had served as the company's president until two months before his death. He had been succeeded in the position by his son, George, Jr.

The obituary went on to list Benson's memberships in a variety of clubs and service organizations, noting that he had been "one of the most respected and well-liked citizens of the community." Perhaps honoring the memory of one of Tyndall's most successful and important businessmen, the article tactfully made no mention of the events that had led to the demise of the Security Bank.

* * *

On Monday, I spent some time at the website of the South Dakota Secretary of State, who was responsible for businesses registered in the state as well as for Elections, Lobbyist Registration, and Pistol Permits. The page offered a link for contacting the office and I filled out a form indicating that I was looking for information about a business that had been incorporated in 1928 and wondering if the records would still be on file with their office.

Next, I went to the John Deere company's website hoping that they might have a company historian or archivist. After searching through several pages, I found a link to the company's history and an email address for the company archives. I sent them a brief message, indicating that I was doing research on South Dakota in the 1920s. I told them that one of my subjects had opened a John Deere dealership in the latter part of the decade, and asked what that might have entailed at the time.

I hit "Send" and returned to my inbox to discover that I'd already received a response from the South Dakota Secretary of State's office. The Business Services Specialist who replied to my email indicated that the office did retain historical records for businesses that were registered with the Secretary of State. She noted that the records prior to 1993 were not available on the internet, but that I could send an email request for the business's information and they could check the files in their archives to see what might be available.

I replied, thanking the woman for her timely response, and indicating that I was looking for whatever information the office might still have regarding the formation of the Benson Farm Implement Company in Tyndall in 1928. In particular, I told her, I would be interested in knowing who the original incorporators might have been, who the members of the company's board of directors were, what the stock structure was, and who the original registered agent had been.

Ten minutes after sending the request, I got a reply indicating that they would check the archives and get back to me. The specialist indicated that it might be a few days before someone would be able to get into the archives and dig out the information. I responded, saying that I was very grateful for the effort and for whatever information they could provide and told them that whenever they could get back to me would be fine.

* * *

I spent another couple of hours poking around on the Internet without learning anything else of much interest. I googled the Bon Homme Heritage Museum in Tyndall, but they apparently didn't have a website and I wasn't able to learn anything about the material they might possess in their collections. I also found the phone number for the Tyndall Public Library. The woman who answered the phone there told me that the library did have virtually a complete collection of the newspapers that were published in Tyndall during the 1920s and '30s. The newspapers were on microfilm, she said, and were not available anywhere online.

I sat back in my desk chair mulling things over for thirty minutes or so and then returned to the internet and looked up flights from Phoenix to Omaha, Nebraska, which appeared to be the nearest city of any size to Tyndall.

I discovered that American had a non-stop flight that left Phoenix at 9:05 a.m. and arrived in Omaha at 1:44 in the afternoon. The round-trip fare seemed reasonable enough, and so I then googled the distance from Omaha to Tyndall, which turned out to be just under two hundred miles via I-29 and South Dakota State Highway 50. I assumed that it would take about three hours to make the drive and that, allowing for time enough to rent a car and have some lunch along the way, I could get to Tyndall between five and six o'clock in the afternoon.

There appeared to be only one motel in Tyndall, a small mom-and-pop operation that was open from 7:00 a.m. to 11:00 p.m. daily and which advertised itself as "a great place to stop and rest." Rooms were available starting at $56.00 per night plus tax. I assumed that four days would certainly be sufficient time to allow me to get a feel for the town and to spend some time in the library and in the museum, and so I reserved a flight for the following Monday morning, returning on Saturday. I then booked a rental car and a room at the motel in Tyndall, thinking that I might have a drink at the Dugout after I checked into the motel on Monday afternoon.

7.

The flight from Sky Harbor in Phoenix to Omaha's Eppley Airfield was uneventful and we arrived ten minutes early. I grabbed a hot dog and a Coke at a bar in the airport, and then stepped out of the terminal into a bright, sunny afternoon with only a handful of puffy white clouds scudding across the sky. The temperature was hovering somewhere in the high nineties, about ten degrees cooler than Phoenix, but the humidity was also in the high nineties and I immediately found myself sweating profusely and missing the dry heat of the Northern Sonoran Desert.

I slipped on my sunglasses and took the shuttle to the rental car center, which was about five minutes away. At the Budget office I filled out the requisite forms and selected a Chrysler 300 as my ride for the next few days. I set my watch for Central Daylight Time, losing two hours out of my day in the process, and then stowed my bag in the trunk.

Once clear of the airport, I headed north on I-29, which almost immediately jogged east into Iowa and then followed the Missouri River north, along the Iowa-Nebraska border. The posted speed limit was 70 MPH, and traffic was very light. I set the cruise control at 79, figuring that if anyone was out patrolling the highway, they'd probably let me slide at that speed.

Through the river valley the countryside was rolling and green, populated with a variety of large trees and shrubs. Off to the east of the Interstate, the land was considerably flatter and consisted of farm fields as far as the eye could see in any direction. Ten days shy of Independence Day, the corn stalks were tall and green and just beginning to tassel. Even with the windows rolled up and the air conditioning running, I could still smell the faint scent of pollen hanging in the air. The soybeans appeared to be doing equally well, and I passed several fields of what I assumed to be spring wheat with a sea of green bearded heads waving gently in the breeze. It appeared that, if the weather cooperated, the area farmers were in for an excellent harvest.

Exits for a few tiny towns appeared at infrequent intervals and then, about an hour and fifteen minutes after leaving the airport, I reached Sioux City, Iowa. The traffic here was fairly congested, due in part, I supposed, to the hour of the day and also to what appeared to be a fairly significant road construction project to widen I-29 as it made its way through the city. After fighting the traffic for fifteen minutes or so, I finally broke free and crossed the border into South Dakota where the speed limit rose to 80 MPH.

I bumped the cruise control to 87 and followed the Interstate for another twenty minutes before reaching Exit 26, which took me onto South Dakota Highway 50 for the last sixty miles into Tyndall. A few miles after leaving the Interstate, I passed through Vermillion. Now moving west from the Missouri River Valley, the land was suddenly as flat as the top of a pool table. Lines of trees appeared here and there, planted, I assumed, years earlier along section lines to act as wind breaks.

A few miles after leaving Vermillion, I passed through Yankton, a larger city than I had anticipated. The speed limit dropped to 35, and traffic was fairly heavy. It took me fifteen or twenty minutes to work my way through the town and at that point, the highway shrunk from four lanes down to two for the rest of the drive to Tyndall. About halfway between Yankton and Tyndall, I drove by a huge field of tan winter wheat. A line of combines was harvesting the crop into a chaser bin. There were no farmhouses or buildings anywhere in sight, and I wondered how many small, one-family farms had ultimately been combined into what I assumed was probably a large corporate farm. Small wonder that rural counties like Bon Homme were still steadily losing population.

Just after five thirty, I passed the "Welcome to Tyndall" sign, which indicated that Tyndall was "A City on the Rise." Two gas station/convenience stores sat at the intersection of the highway and Tyndall's Main Street, and a bit further down the highway, I could see a Dollar Store and a Chevy dealership.

I turned right onto Main Street and drove for several blocks through a residential area. The houses varied both in age and appearance; some were very well-tended while others clearly needed attention. The street was lined with trees and the lots seemed generous in size. Most of the houses had fairly large lawns.

After a few blocks, the residential area gave way to the business district. At the south end of the district, I found the Welcome Inn Motel stretched out behind a broad expanse of grass that separated it from the street. The place was a one-story structure that appeared to date from sometime in the middle of the last century. I counted twenty rooms, with space enough for cars to park on the broad gravel drive that fronted them. Judging by the number of vehicles that were parked in front, it appeared that the motel was about a third full for the evening.

In the office, the owner/manager checked me in and welcomed me to Tyndall. He asked what brought me to town and I told him that I was researching my family's history, but when I told him my mother's maiden name, it apparently meant nothing to him. He handed me an old-fashioned key to the room, one which was hanging off a plastic tag with the unit number, the name and address of the motel and a guarantee that the motel would pay the postage if the key were dropped into any mailbox.

Back in the car, I drove the thirty yards to my room, and parked in front of the unit. The room itself was fairly small, but clean and neat. A sign on the back of the door noted that rags were available in the office and asked that guests not use the towels in the room for "cleaning cars, boots, guns, etc."

It seemed a fair request, and I dropped my suitcase on the bed, used the bathroom, then went back out to the Chrysler and headed north up Main Street. The business district appeared to extend for about five or six blocks. Most of the buildings were obviously decades old, although there were a few that appeared to be more recent. A number of the buildings appeared to be empty and I also saw a few vacant spaces where the buildings that once stood there had obviously been torn town.

I found the Dugout toward the north end of town on the corner of Main Street and Seventeenth Avenue. Just east of the building and across the street was a large grain elevator, which appeared to be the tallest structure in town. North and west, a bright blue water tower with the town's name emblazoned across it, poked out above the trees.

The Dugout appeared to be exactly as advertised in the photo on the town's website. I stood for a moment at the front door, then drew a deep breath, pulled the door open, and walked in. The space immediately beyond the door was maybe twenty-five feet square, with several tables and chairs positioned in front of a U-shaped bar that effectively divided the room at that point. A couple of stands holding small bags of chips and other snacks anchored each end of the bar and several napkin holders and salt and pepper shakers lined the space between them.

A dozen stools were arranged around the bar, two of which were occupied by an elderly couple drinking Budweisers out of the bottle. Behind the bar was a large cooler with glass doors that revealed a variety of beers and a few bottles of white wine. A small TV, muted and tuned to ESPN, hung above the cooler, and a string of tiny white lights had been draped along the back wall. A few more signs advertising a variety of beers also hung on the back wall, and a door in the middle of the wall opened into what was, apparently, the kitchen. At the end of the bar on my left, a short hallway led to the unisex restroom. On the right, a row of booths upholstered in black vinyl to match the bar stools, lined the wall.

A heavyset man wearing tan shorts and a salmon-colored golf shirt stood behind the bar, watching me as I walked in and surveyed the room. Somewhere in his middle forties, his face was lightly tanned, save for his forehead, which I assumed was protected by a cap when he was outside in the sun. He was sporting a small circle beard on a face that was otherwise closely shaved. As I approached the bar, he gave me a smile and said, "What can I do you for?"

I took a stool, leaving one empty seat between myself and the elderly couple, and ordered an MGD. The 'tender pulled one from the cooler, popped the top, and set the beer in front of me without asking me whether I might want a glass to go with it. I took a long pull on the beer, which tasted especially good after the long drive, and he asked me where I was from.

"Just in from Phoenix," I said, "visiting for a couple of days."

"Really? What brings you up to Tyndall?"

"My family used to live up here, and I just wanted to visit the town and do a little genealogical research."

The guy stuck out his hand and said, "I'm Matt; I own the place."

"Jack Oliva," I said, shaking his hand.

I took another sip of the beer, looked around the room, and said, "Do you know anything about the history of this building from when it used to be a bank?"

The guy gave me another big smile. "Oh hell, yeah. In fact, this may be the most famous building in Tyndall."

"How's that?"

"Well, back in the 1920s, the bank that was in this building went bust because one of the cashiers stole a ton of money. And then, when he got caught, rather than go to jail, he shot himself right back there in the room where the kitchen is now."

I set my beer on the bar and looked up at the guy. "Well, as it happens, the man who shot himself back there was my grandfather."

If I'd never before understood the concept of someone's jaw dropping, I did in that moment. The man's eyes widened, and he took a step back from the bar, staring at me in apparent disbelief. Then he turned back in the direction of the kitchen and shouted, "Bob, get the hell out here. The ghost's grandson is sitting at the bar!"

I shot the guy a look and a moment later another man, younger and thinner, but looking every bit as much surprised, stepped out of the kitchen. The bartender pointed at me, and the two of them stood there looking at me slack jawed. In the meantime, the couple sitting at the bar had turned and were appraising me with the same amazed expression on their faces.

I finally broke the silence and said, "What the hell do you mean, the ghost's grandson?"

The bartender shook his head and pointed back toward the kitchen. "Well, ever since it happened, people have sworn that this building is haunted by the ghost of the man who killed himself in there. I swear to God I've heard him moving around in here myself late at night. You're really his grandson?"

"Well, I don't believe in ghosts, but I really am the grandson of the man who died in this building in 1925."

"Holy shit," the guy said, "I just can't believe it."

He turned and pulled another MGD from the cooler, popped the top and set it in front of me. Then he walked around the bar and said, "C'mere here and take a look at this."

He led me over to the long wall on the right and showed me a picture that had been enlarged, framed and hung in the middle of the wall. It showed the interior of the bank with the tellers' cages on a line approximately where the bar now sat, and the vault, with the large door standing open, immediately behind the tellers' cages.

A man and a woman, both of whom appeared to be in their middle thirties, were sitting at a desk in front of the cages, facing the camera. And standing behind them, leaning casually against one of the teller's cages, was an older man, perhaps in his late forties, with a mustache and thinning hair. His right arm was braced against a pillar at the end of the row of tellers' windows; his left was bent at the elbow with his fist resting against his waist. He looked to be a bit overweight and was dressed in dark slacks, a white shirt with suspenders, and a tie that was tucked into the shirt. He stood, staring directly into the camera's lens, a self-confident man of the world.

The bartender pointed at the picture and in an excited voice he said, "This is the guy." Pointing to a spot in the middle of the room, he continued, "This picture was taken right there just a year or so before it happened."

In a smaller framed photo, hanging just below the larger one, the same man was captured sitting at a desk and signing some documents. I would have never recognized him from the photo that was sitting on my desk back home in Phoenix, but sixteen years down the road, my grandfather would have obviously aged, and I had no reason to doubt the bartender's story.

In the wake of his exuberance, the bartender finally realized the gravity of the moment, at least as far as I was concerned, and he stepped back a bit and stood quietly, clasping his arms behind his back as I contemplated the pictures. Finally, I turned and said, "Would you mind if we set these pictures on the table over there so that I could take a couple of photos of them?"

"No, of course not. Absolutely!"

With that, he took the larger picture off the wall and set it on the table. I pulled my phone from my pocket, took several different shots of the picture, and then checked to see that I had at least a couple of good ones. We then repeated the process with the smaller picture and the bartender hung them back on the wall. We retreated to our positions on each side of the bar, and the guy stood there shaking his head. "Man, this is so weird; I just can't believe it."

I took a pull on the second beer and said, "How long have you been in this spot?"

"A little over three years. There've been four or five businesses in and out of here over the years, and the place has sat empty for a long time in between. People keep saying that the building's been cursed ever since the bank went under and the cashier died in here. I'm hoping that's not really the case," he said, tapping his knuckles against the top of the wooden bar, "and so far, at least, we've been doing okay."

Nodding back in the direction of the photos on the wall, I said, "Do you know if there are any other pictures from back when this was the bank?

He shook his head. "Not as far as I know. I found those two buried back in the storeroom when I rented the place and so I hung them up on the wall. I've never seen any others, but I s'pose there might be some over at the museum."

"Do you know if there are any Kratinas still around here? I believe that my grandfather moved here from Nebraska to join his sister's family, but I checked the local phone books online and didn't find a reference to anyone by that name."

He thought about it for a few seconds and then shook his head again. "Nope. The only Kratina I ever heard of was your grandfather. I grew up and went to school here and never ran into anybody by that name."

"My grandmother's maiden name was Sedlaceck. That ring any bells?"

'No, sorry."

"That's okay. I couldn't find any of them on the Internet either and there didn't appear to be any of them still around by the time the 1940 census was taken, but I thought I'd ask."

"Well, as I understand it a lot of people moved out of this county during the Depression. Maybe the rest of your relatives decided to move on to greener pastures."

"Maybe."

I drained the last of the second beer and said, "Well, thanks for the information and for letting me copy the pictures. I'm sure I'll see you again before I leave."

I reached for my wallet, but the bartender shook his head and said, "Don't worry about it, man. Those are on the house. Come back any time."

I nodded my thanks and got up from the stool, taking a long look over the bar into the small space where my grandfather had died. Then I thanked the guy again and walked slowly back through the door and out into the early evening.

8.

It was now a little after six o'clock, and the only thing I'd had to eat all day was the hot dog in Omaha. I was ready for some dinner but, all things considered, I decided that I didn't want it coming from the kitchen of the Dugout.

The temperature had cooled a little and so I decided to leave my car parked where it was and make a brief circuit of the business district. I headed south down Main Street for a couple of blocks, then crossed the street and headed back north up the west side of the street. Only a handful of cars were parked along the street, and there was no traffic at all save for a woman who passed me heading south down the street on her John Deere riding lawn mower.

About halfway up the street, I passed a bowling alley that also apparently featured a café. The windows were covered and when I tried the door, it was locked. I couldn't be sure if it was simply closed for the evening or closed for good.

At 20th Avenue, I crossed back over to the east side of the street and headed south again. Just before reaching the Dugout, I found a small café, which was apparently the only other place to eat in Tyndall, apart from the convenience stores out where Main Street met the highway. It appeared to be doing a reasonably good dinnertime business, and taking that as a good sign, I stepped through the door.

The right side of the café was lined with booths, upholstered in tan vinyl. A row of tables ran down the center of the room and on the left was a traditional diner counter with round stools upholstered to match the booths on the other side of the room. Four ceiling fans rotated slowly above the diners.

I took a seat in an empty booth toward the middle of the restaurant, and a few of the customers looked over in my direction, obviously curious about the presence of a stranger in town. A couple of them acknowledged me with a tip of the head and a slight smile, and then turned back to their dinners.

A young waitress who might have been fifteen or sixteen appeared with a smile, a menu and a glass of water. She asked if I'd like something to drink and, since the place apparently didn't serve alcohol, I ordered a Coke. She made a note on a small pad and told me that she'd be right back to take my order.

The menu was exactly what one might have expected in a small-town café in the middle of farm country. The most exotic dinner choice available appeared to be Beef Stroganoff, and after glancing over the menu I settled on Chicken Fried Steak, which I assumed would be a staple in a place like this and something that they'd probably do pretty well.

The girl returned with my Coke, and fifteen minutes later she was back with the Chicken Fried Steak. It was a very generous serving, smothered in cream gravy, and accompanied by mashed potatoes that were obviously homemade and not out of a box or can. Suddenly feeling ravenously hungry, I tucked into the dinner which turned out to be excellent and very filling. When I was finished, the waitress returned, cleared the empty plate, and said, "Did you save room for some dessert? My aunt makes the best pies in the state."

I shook my head. "That sounds fantastic, but that was a great dinner and a lot of it. I don't know where I'd put any pie at this point. But I'll be sure to stop in tomorrow and try some."

"We'll be here," she said, offering another big smile.

She left the check and I covered it with cash, leaving a generous tip. I then walked back to my car and spent thirty minutes or so driving up and down the streets of the town, trying to get a feel for the lay of the land. The town was laid out on a grid with the streets all running due north and south or east and west. Virtually all of the businesses were located along Main Street, and from there, residential neighborhoods extended another few blocks in every direction.

While there were some newer homes scattered here and there, most of the houses all appeared to be several decades old. In some cases, people had added rooms and made other renovations that were obviously more recent, but the overall effect was that of a small rural town, clinging as best it could to the population and the economic activity that it still had left. As along Main Street, the residential lots appeared to be very generous with lots of trees and large lawns. Many of the side streets off of Main were fairly narrow and appeared to be of oil and chip construction.

Several people were out mowing their lawns as I drove by and I saw a number of others sitting outside in lawn chairs enjoying the evening. On the west side of town I found a large city park with a lake, a swimming pool, a baseball field and some playground equipment.

As the photo on the town's website suggested, the Benson Farm Implement Company appeared to be easily the most prosperous business in town. A large building that was almost square sat in the middle of a graveled lot at the far north end of Main Street. The sales office ran along the front of the building, and several huge doors along its south side suggested that the service center was located there.

Several tractors and several other pieces of equipment, including brands other than John Deere, were arranged on the lot in front of the building and appeared to consist of both new and used inventory. At first glance, the inventory appeared to be smaller than I would have expected, but it then occurred to me that, in this day and age, most new agricultural equipment would probably be special ordered and configured to meet the needs of the specific customer.

I circled the block, taking the measure of the place, which seemed somehow out of synch with the older and much smaller businesses in town, then turned south back down Main Street. It was now heading toward nine o'clock and the sun was setting rapidly. I decided I'd done about all I could for the evening and so headed back to the Welcome Inn and climbed into bed with John Sandford's new Virgil Flowers novel. I read several chapters and then turned out the light, determined to get a good night's sleep so that I'd be ready to go bright and early in the morning.

9.

I woke up a little after seven and lay in bed for a couple of minutes while I planned out my day. Then I got up, shaved, showered, and dressed in a tee shirt, a pair of good jeans, and my vintage Stan Smiths.

I've never been much of a breakfast guy, but I did want a cup of coffee to get the day started and so I drove back up to the café and took a stool at the counter. The place was about three-quarters full, with a crowd that consisted mostly of farmers and other guys who looked like they were on their way to work. A couple of tables were occupied by men who were considerably older and who looked like they might well be retired, but who were still starting their day as they probably had for years, having breakfast in the café and catching up on the local news and gossip.

The coffee was hot, black and strong—no Caramel Brulee Lattés, Espresso Macchiatos, Java Chip Frappuccinos or Iced Peppermint Mocha Grandes on the menu here. The "barista" — Meg, by her name tag—was somewhere in her late forties, a sassy Bottle Blonde with bright green eyes and a very appealing Rubenesque figure that was tucked into a pair of jeans shorts and a dark blue tee shirt. She looked like she'd been waiting on these guys for a good many years and like she probably knew most, if not all, of their secrets. There was an easy rapport among the diners and between them and the two waitresses. I appeared to be the only person in the place who hadn't been breakfasting there for years, and as had been the case last night, I drew a few curious glances.

I drained the last of the coffee, paid, thanked the waitress, and then drove on up the street to the County Sheriff's Department.

The office was in the courthouse, a three-story granite building which, according to the plaque on the wall outside, had been built in 1914. Inside I found a century-old building that looked like it had been renovated any number of times through the years to meet changing times and circumstances. The result was a curious mishmash which suggested that the building had been cobbled together by several different architects who couldn't agree about exactly what they were attempting to accomplish.

I found the Sheriff's office on the first floor with a young female deputy staffing the front desk. She finished typing a line on the report she was writing, then looked up and said, "Good morning. Can I help you?"

"Well, I'm not sure," I replied. "I'm in town for a couple of days from Arizona doing some genealogical research on my family who lived in Tyndall in the 1920s. I was just wondering if your records might go back that far."

She smiled and shook her head. "I'm afraid not. To be honest, well into the 1950s, this was still a very small department and the record keeping was pretty informal. The States Attorney's Office would probably still have records of cases that they took to trial, and the Clerk of the Court's Office might have records of trials going back that far, but the sheriffs back then kept their own records and took them with them with they left the office."

"So, if I'm understanding you correctly, the records of any investigations from back then would only still exist if first the sheriff and then his descendants had hung onto them all this time?"

"I'm afraid that's it. Was there a particular case you were interested in?"

"My grandfather, Charles Kratina, died as a suicide here in 1925. I'm assuming that when his body was discovered, the sheriff would have been called and would have conducted at least a minimal investigation to determine what had happened. I knew that the chance was small, of course, but I was hoping that there might still be some official record of the investigation around somewhere."

Again, she shook her head. "Nope, sorry. I wish I could help..."

"Can you tell me who the sheriff was in 1925?"

She opened a desk drawer and pulled out a blue binder with the County Sheriff's badge on the cover. She flipped open the binder and ran her finger down a list of names on the first page. Still looking at the list, she said, "That would have been Hal Howard, who served from 1918 until January 1926. He was replaced by Gary Checka who served from 1926 until 1940."

I made a note of the names and said, "Do you know if either man might still have family in this general area?"

"No, sorry, I don't. Neither of the names means anything to me, but of course, either man could have had daughters whose descendants still live around here but with different last names."

"I suppose. Oh well, as I said, I knew that it would probably be a long shot, but I still wanted to check."

"That's fine; sorry I couldn't be more help."

I thanked the deputy, left the office, and walked upstairs to the office of the Register of Deeds. A shapely woman with grey hair but who didn't look to be any older than her late forties or early fifties was working at a desk behind the counter. When I walked through the door, she came over to the counter and asked if she could be of help.

"I hope so. I'm doing some genealogical research on my family. My grandparents lived in Tyndall through the middle 1920s, and the census indicates that they owned a home on State Street. I was hoping that I might be able to see the house where they lived and wondered if your records might go back far enough to show the address."

"Oh yes. Our records from back then aren't computerized, but I can look it up for you."

The woman wrote down my grandfather's name, which seemed to mean no more to her than it had to the owner of the Welcome Inn or to the young sheriff's deputy. She walked over to a bank of file cabinets and pulled out a large ledger book. She flipped past several pages, then stopped and began running her finger down the page. Holding her spot on the page with a finger on her left hand, she picked up a pen with her right and made a note on the slip of paper on which she had written my grandfather's name.

She closed the ledger, slipped it back into the file cabinet and went back to her desk. There she massaged her computer keyboard for a couple of minutes before coming back over to the counter. She passed the slip of paper over to me and said, "The records indicate that Charles Kratina owned a home at 1710 State Street from April 1915, until June of 1930. At that point, the house was sold to someone named Jackson, and there have been three other owners since then. The property now belongs to a couple who bought it in 2002."

The woman told me how to find the house, which was only a few blocks away from the courthouse, and explained that since some of the street names in the town had been changed, State Street was now Laurel. I thanked her for her help and went back out to my rental car. Five minutes later, I was parked in front of a white two-story clapboard house that looked to have been painted very recently. The yard was neatly trimmed, and a variety of flowers and shrubs had been planted in beds in front of the house. Behind the house was a two-car garage that was obviously only a few years old and painted to match the house. A large boat, covered by a tarp, sat on a slab next to the garage.

I sat there for several minutes, staring at the house where my mother had lived as a child, trying to imagine what her life might have been like in that house and how it might have been changed had my grandfather not decided to help himself to $200,000 of the Security Bank's money.

Every life ultimately turns on an infinite number of decisions and actions, many of which we don't necessarily have a chance to make for ourselves. And sitting there, it occurred to me that had my grandfather not decided first to embezzle all that money and then to kill himself, he and his family might have continued to live in this house and in this town for years. My grandmother would have never moved to Montana; my mother would have never met my father, and I would not exist.

The consequences of my grandfather's actions had radiated out from that tiny bank on Main Street to ultimately impact the lives of thousands of people, even down to the present day, and it was sobering to think of all the grief and pain that my mother, her brothers, my grandmother, and doubtless a lot of other people had to endure so that I might ultimately come into the world.

10.

It was now eleven-thirty and after skipping breakfast, I decided it was time for lunch. I drove back up to the café and again took a seat at the counter. Meg, the waitress who had been there earlier in the morning, was still on duty and welcomed me back. Remembering last night's advice from the young waitress, I ordered a BLT and a Coke.

The sandwich was excellent, with thick bacon, a ripe, juicy tomato, crisp romaine, and bread that appeared to be homemade, perhaps from the Tyndall Bakery next door to the café. I took my time, enjoying every bite, and then, when the waitress cleared my plate, I ordered a piece of apple pie for dessert. Standing there holding the plate, she said "Do you want me to warm that up a bit and maybe put some ice cream with it?"

"I'm in your hands. Serve it the way you think best."

Five minutes later, she was back with a thick slice of pie with a delicate flaky crust and tender, delicious apples that were seasoned with just the right amount of cinnamon and nutmeg. The waitress stood by with her hand on her hip while I took the first bite and then said, "Well?"

I swallowed and looked across the counter at her. "I think I'm going to be moving to Tyndall. Do you know of any homes for sale up here and are you by any chance single?"

She shook her head and laughed. "I'm sure you'd be a welcome addition to the town, and the answer to both of your questions is yes."

She stuck out her hand and said, "Meg. And I suppose if we're going to be an item, I ought to at least know your name."

I laughed, shook her hand and said, "Jack Oliva. Nice to meet you, Meg."

"What brings you to town, Jack?"

"My family lived here back in the Twenties. I'm up for a few days, doing some research into the family's history."

She thought for a moment, then shook her head. "I don't know that I ever heard of any Olivas around here."

"It was my mother's family that lived here. Their name was Kratina."

Now she nodded. "That does sound familiar."

She hesitated, the wheels clearly turning in her mind. Then she looked over my shoulder at a table of three men across the room and said, "Bud?"

A heavyset man, maybe in his middle fifties, wearing jeans, a white oxford shirt, and a cap that read "Wyffels Hybrids" looked up from his soup and said, "What, Darlin'?"

"Don't you have some Kratinas back up your family tree somewhere?"

"My gramma," he replied. "Why're you askin'?"

She pointed at me and said, "I think you and Jack here might be related."

The guy gave her a look as if she might be joking with him, and when he realized that she wasn't, he got up from the table and walked across the room. The waitress pointed from me to him and back to me again. "Jack, Bud; Bud, Jack. You guys figure this out; I've got work to do."

He took the stool next to me and I offered my hand. "Jack Oliva."

He gave me a firm handshake and said, "Bud Daniels. So why the hell does Meg think we might be related?"

"You said your grandmother was a Kratina?"

He nodded and I said, "Well, so was my grandfather. He and his family lived here in the 1920s."

The guy appeared to be even more surprised than the bartender had been last night. "Your grandad was Charles Kratina?"

"Yes, he was."

"Holy shit. My gramma was his younger sister, which must make us second cousins or some such thing."

I nodded. "You know, truth to tell, I've never really been able to sort all of that out much past first cousins. What do you do up here, Bud?"

"I'm farming the land that originally belonged to my great-grandfather, just north of town. And you?"

"I'm a retired police detective from Phoenix. And believe it or not, I knew nothing at all about my grandfather—not even his name—until four weeks ago. My mom died a couple of months ago, and I found a picture of him in a box that she'd put away for years. I got curious about the guy and after doing what research I could on the Internet, I decided to come up here to see what else I might learn."

"So, by now of course, you know what happened to him?"

"Oh, yeah. It was a shock, believe me. But it explains why my mother and grandmother never talked about him."

He nodded. "Yeah, well, a lot of people around here suffered quite a bit as a result of all that business, including my gramma. Some people, even a few of her friends, just turned around and flat froze her out, as if she had any damned thing to do with what happened."

"That had to be tough."

"No doubt. It got a bit better as time went on. Some of those people moved away when things really turned sour here in the thirties, and of course the ones who stayed gradually began to die off. But there were still a couple of families who wouldn't give my dad the time of day when he was growing up.

"Speaking of which," he said, looking down at his watch, "I really would like to talk some with you; it's not every day you get to meet a new cousin. But I've got an appointment over at the bank in like four and a half minutes, and I need to get my butt on down there. Tell you what, Jack, why don't you come on out for supper tomorrow tonight?"

"Thanks, Bud, I appreciate the offer, but I don't want to intrude into your evening or cause you and your family any inconvenience."

"Aw bullshit, cousin, we're family!" He laughed and said, "Really, Jack, it would be fun to get to know you a bit, and my wife always cooks a ton of good food. Please, come on out."

"Well, if you're sure..."

"I'm sure."

He gave me his cell phone number and quickly wrote down the directions to his farm, saying that it would take me about fifteen minutes to get there from town. "Come about six, and for god's sake, don't dress up in anything more formal than what you've got on right now. We'll sit on the porch and have a beer or maybe two and then eat around seven or so."

I thanked him and slipped the note with the directions into my pocket. We shook hands again and he looked over at the waitress. "Meg, Sweetie, I'm out of here. Give the check to Curt today."

"Will do, Hon," she replied. "You have a good one."

I watched him hurry out the door, savored the last few bites of my pie, and then said, "I need to get going too, Meg. What do I owe you?"

She gave me the check and we settled up. As I got up off the stool, she offered another smile and said, "Good to see you again, Jack. Don't be a stranger."

11.

The Tyndall Public Library was open for only a few hours in the afternoon from Tuesday through Friday each week. At one o'clock, I was standing at the front door when the librarian appeared with the key to open for the afternoon. After talking to her on the phone, I'd been expecting to see a stereotypical small-town librarian—a woman probably in her middle sixties with her gray hair gathered back into a bun. Consequently, I was surprised to see that, instead, she was an attractive brunette, stylishly dressed, and somewhere in her early forties.

The red brick building was obviously decades old and looked and smelled exactly like the libraries I had loved back when I was a kid. Dark wooden shelves filled with books lined the walls, and substantial chairs and tables that looked to be made of oak were positioned around the room. I stood there, taking in the place as the woman moved through the room turning on the lights. "I love your library," I said. "They don't build them like this anymore."

"Thanks," she said, "I love it too. It's a Carnegie library, built in 1917. Much of the furniture is still original."

She told me a bit more about the building and its history and then asked how she could be of help. I explained that I was interested in looking at the town's newspapers from 1925, and she set me up at a microfilm reader with a roll that contained the *Tyndall Register* from December of 1921 to September of 1927.

It was a weekly newspaper, published on Thursdays, and devoted entirely to community events. A subscription cost two dollars a year. Scanning a few issues, I found no reference to any state or national events. A typical issue from January 1922, featured a front-page article titled "The Farmer's Wife," which offered helpful advice for packing your child's school lunch so that it would remain "fresh and tasty."

Otherwise, the paper contained human interest stories, a couple of "Tall Tales," and a few articles about agriculture. Much of the paper was devoted to the comings and goings of the local population, and I learned that on Monday evening, Miss Ella Sratka had returned from a short visit with friends at Sioux City. Meanwhile, H. L. Brelsferd had informed the editor that "the ice harvest would not start this week as planned as the ice was barely six inches thick."

Advertisers included the local funeral home, a Kodak photo finishing store, livestock auctioneers, a meat market, the Tyndall Bakery and a veterinarian. The paper also published the professional cards of a few attorneys, doctors and dentists. There was apparently one movie house in town, the Cozy Theatre, and their ad indicated that on January 5th and 6th, they would be showing "Unguarded Women," staring Bebe Daniels and Richard Dix. The ad noted that the movie was a story of "a modern, jazz-wild girl and a man's unselfish attempt to reform her."

It occurred to me that the movie would have been released before the introduction of the Hayes Code in 1927, which was designed to tame the movie industry, and I wondered just how "modern" and "jazz-wild" the heroine of the film might have been.

Scrolling through the issues, I saw several ads for the Security Bank, encouraging people to practice thrift and to open checking and savings accounts. At the bottom of every ad was the bank's slogan, "There Is No Substitute for Safety." There was apparently only one other bank in town, the First National Bank, which advertised much along the same lines.

It seemed clear that, even this early, the agricultural depression that began in 1921 was already taking its toll. Each edition of the *Register* contained notices of mortgage and foreclosure sales.

There were also ads advertising farm auctions as failing farmers surrendered to the economic realities and abandoned their lands.

There appeared to be very little crime, although the issue of February 5, 1922, reported that a man had been arrested for forgery and for stealing a car. Later in the month, someone broke into Tony's restaurant and stole three hundred dollars' worth of cigarettes. I had no idea what a pack of cigarettes might have cost in 1922, but it couldn't have been all that much, and it struck me that the thief must have gotten away with quite a haul.

Mid-February was apparently a hazardous time to be living in and around Tyndall, and the paper reported that "Lloyd Peterson is carrying his finger in a sling these days on account of having broken it with too strenuous playing of basketball Monday night. Leo Kiehlbauch is also limping around for the same reason." If that weren't bad enough, "Prof. Evert, while skating on the ice last Sunday, fell, striking his head on the ice so hard that he was unconscious for several hours. He is all right again, taking care of his school duties."

Relieved to know that the professor was back on the job, I wound the film forward to 1925. When I reached the editions for May, I slowed down and began reading more carefully. Nothing out of the ordinary appeared to have occurred during the first three weeks of the month, but then I got to the issue for May 20, and saw the headline announcing that "Chas. Kratina Commits Suicide This Morning. Left a Note Apologizing for Wrong-Doing."

The article then went on to report the basic facts of the situation that I had found earlier in the *Argus Leader.* The paper noted that another employee had arrived at the bank and "was compelled to unlock the door, which was rather unusual as Mr. Kratina always had the bank open before anyone else arrived. On entering the vault, he found Mr. Kratina lying next to a stool, having shot himself in the neck. The sheriff and the coroner were called, and the remains were taken to the Eggers undertaking parlors."

Also, on the front page, the paper published a letter from the president of the bank, addressed to "Patrons of the Security Bank of Tyndall." The president noted that during the nearly fifty years of its existence, the bank's management "has always adhered to the strict rules of conservative banking," and that the bank "has passed successfully through many financial depressions and has emerged from the recent financial collapse as one of the leading institutions of the state."

Sadly, "the management of the bank now greatly regrets to inform its patrons that due to bad management on the part of its assistant cashier, certain checks were cashed by him which were later found to be spurious and probably worthless, and it is now doubtful that anything can be realized on them. Immediately upon the discovery of the probable loss, the Bank directors met, and the amount apparently lost was immediately made good by the directors."

The letter went on to state that a new assistant cashier had been appointed and expressed the hope that the confidence of the public in the bank, "would not be shaken by this one incident. The management conscientiously believes that the bank is as strong and safe as at any time in its history."

I couldn't help but wonder how confident the president and the board of directors really were. Obviously, they were trying to contain any potential panic that might precipitate a run on the bank and cause it to fail, but did they really believe at this point that they could still keep the bank afloat?

Moving forward a week, the edition of May 28 included a front-page headline which read, "Chas. Kratina Buried in Czech Cemetery."

The story went on to note that the service had been held in the family home. A man named Richard Wilberforce conducted the service and a large crowd attended. The town firemen turned out in uniform, and at the conclusion of the funeral, they marched with the body of their former chief to the cemetery northeast of town. The paper's editor joined "the many, many friends in expressing sympathy to the bereaved family."

The issue also contained a note from my grandmother, thanking the members of the community for their support and noting that, "The tender sympathy of our friends has greatly helped us to bear our grief."

In a separate article, the paper noted that the bank's president, C. G. Webster, and the head cashier, George Benson, had been in Sioux Falls on May 18 and 19, meeting with state banking regulators. They returned to Tyndall on the afternoon of the 20th and were said to be "badly shocked" by the news of what had transpired in their absence. The paper quoted Webster, who said, somewhat enigmatically, only that "Mr. Katrina had been with the bank for a number of years. We extend our deepest sympathies to his family."

My grandparents were Catholics, and I noted that the service had been conducted at my grandparents' home and by a layman, rather than being held at St. Leo's, the local Catholic church, with a funeral mass celebrated by a priest. My grandfather had then been buried in the Czech National Cemetery, rather than in the town's Catholic cemetery. I assumed that this reflected the church's conviction, apparently firmly enforced in this case, that suicide was a mortal sin and that someone who took his own life could not be buried in hallowed Catholic ground.

The paper's next issue, dated June 4, announced in bold headlines that "Security Bank Closes Doors: Will organize new bank as soon as arrangements can be made—from Four to Six Weeks."

The article then went on to say that on the previous Monday morning, a sign had been posted on the door of the bank, notifying the public that the bank was closed and was now in the hands of the State Banking Department. "There had been rumors that there were certain irregularities in the bank," the paper reported, and the bank's president had been summoned to Sioux Falls to discuss the issue with state bank examiners.

It initially appeared that the shortage amounted to $48,000, and after an emergency meeting of the bank's board of directors on May 17th, three of the directors agreed to make up the shortage out of their own funds. However, further examination of the situation by the state banking department revealed that the losses were much greater. The bank examiners concluded that once the news broke, "there would no doubt be a run on the bank, and it would be compelled to close. In order to pay the depositors, it was thought best to close the bank and reorganize and open a new one."

The story then went on to describe the fraud that had been perpetrated, naming my grandfather as the party principally responsible for the bank's collapse. In addition to the worthless checks that had previously been discovered, the losses also included about $150,000 in missing certificates of deposit.

Allegedly, my grandfather's partner in crime had come into the bank on several occasions through the spring of 1925 and bought CDs. The bank apparently had several books of them, and instead of simply selling the next certificate in the current book, my grandfather would take a certificate from the last book that the bank had—one that, theoretically, the bank might not get to for years to come.

My grandfather made no entry of the sale in the bank's records and apparently hoped that no one would notice the missing CDs. His accomplice paid for the CDs with checks from out of state banks, and when the checks were returned unpaid, my grandfather simply destroyed them. The newspaper article did not identify the accomplice and did not speculate about what might have become of the money. I assumed that the accomplice had gotten away with it and wondered if my grandfather might have been duped into participating in the scheme only to have been cheated out of his share of the proceeds by his confederate.

In another column in the June 4 edition, the editor noted that "Francis Kratina commenced work on Monday morning at the Hoch Drug Store and is found behind the fountain each day. 'Frank,' as the boys call him, is a very agreeable and accommodating young boy, and we predict success for him."

Francis Kratina would have been my Uncle Frank, my mother's eldest brother, fifteen years old on the day of his father's death. I wondered about the timing of his employment. Was this a summer job that he would have worked under normal circumstances between the school years, or was this, perhaps, an early sign of the desperate economic circumstances in which my grandmother's family had been left?

The paper's next issue on June 11, described the steps that were being taken to reorganize and reopen the bank. It indicated that the name of the reorganized bank would be the "Bank of Tyndall," and that the State Security Commission would meet on June 15 to consider a charter for the bank. The paper noted that approval of the charter would be contingent on a guarantee that, over a period of years, the charter's holders would repay the depositors of the Security Bank the money they had lost. With irony apparently unintended, the directors promised "to make the Bank of Tyndall as strong and as reliable as the old Security Bank."

Reading the next several issues of the paper, though, it became clear that the effort to reorganize the bank had failed, and the Security Bank went into receivership. State banking regulators took control of the institution and began liquidating its assets so that the bank's depositors would ultimately get at least some of their money back. It appeared, though, that those efforts were still underway at the end of 1925, and that the people who had deposited their money in the bank were still waiting to get back even a small portion of their savings.

I could easily understand why a lot of people would have turned against my grandfather's family as a consequence. Back in the day before the federal government insured banking deposits, people who entrusted their money to a bank had little or no recourse if the bank failed and their money was lost; they were simply out of luck. As in this case, the bank's remaining assets would be liquidated, and the proceeds ultimately divided among its creditors. But this would take time, and, almost certainly, none of the depositors would ever make a complete recovery. And in the meantime, for those farmers, merchants and others who were operating on a narrow margin, the loss might well have been serious enough to drive them out of business.

I was sitting there thinking about all of this when my phone dinged, indicating that I had an email message. I opened it to find a response from the Secretary of State's office regarding my inquiry about the Benson Farm Implement Company. The Business Services Specialist apologized for the delay in getting back to me and reported that the company had been incorporated on May 3, 1928.

One hundred shares had been issued, and ninety of them were owned by George Benson. Five shares were owned by Mrs. Ellen Benson, and the other five were owned by Ted Grimke, whose name meant nothing to me. The registered agent was George Benson who was also listed as the president of the corporation. The two Bensons and Grimke constituted the Board of Directors, and Grimke was listed as the vice-president.

George Benson was clearly the principal figure in the company, and I assumed he had parted with only enough shares to create the board of directors. I imagined that the board met infrequently, probably only as often as required by law, and probably only long enough to ratify the decisions that Benson had already made.

I wondered what would have prompted Benson to buy out a farm implement dealership in the middle of an agricultural depression, when most of his customers would almost certainly have to buy his products and services on credit. Where did he get that kind of faith in the future? And where did he get that kind of money?

* * *

I returned to the newspaper and read through the rest of 1925, but it was hard to tell from that how serious the effects of the bank's failure might have been for the community. The paper's editor was clearly a local booster who attempted to put a positive spin on most developments, portraying Tyndall and the surrounding county in the best possible light. Outside of the legal notices regarding mortgage foreclosures and the ads for farm auctions, there was little in the paper to indicate that an agricultural depression was gripping South Dakota and the rest of the nation as well.

The depression apparently *was* causing at least some readers to be delinquent in paying for their subscriptions to the *Register* however, and in one edition the editor noted that, "We sent out a bunch of subscription statements the last of the month and have had excellent results, but there are a number more that should pay at this time as we are in much need of money."

Meanwhile, in the paper's columns, Miss Dupont continued to offer "Advice to Foolish Wives," including such nuggets as, "Your husband will never outgrow the boy stage. Treat him as such and he'll cuddle like an infant." Also: "If he says he's been at the lodge, believe him. You won't add to your peace of mind by learning different." Along apparently similar lines, the Cozy Theatre was featuring Lewis Stone and Helen Chadwick, starring in "Why Men Leave Home," a movie advertised as "a picture which also tells how to keep them there."

The July 23rd edition featured a notice of a hearing regarding a petition for "Letters of Administration in the Matter of the Estate of Charles Katrina, Deceased," in which my grandmother requested that letters of administration of my grandfather's estate be issued to her. The hearing was set for August 11. That same edition featured an article titled "Public Funds Tied Up," indicating that Bon Homme County had $90,740 tied up in failed banks. Of that amount $39,696 had been entrusted to the failed Security Bank of Tyndall. I assumed that the county's budget would not have been all that large to begin with and that having so much money unavailable would have put a serious strain on the county's finances.

After the summer of 1925, the paper made no further reference either to my grandfather's crime or to the bank's failure. If my grandfather's accomplice was ever identified or if any of the money had ever been recovered, the news didn't make it to the pages of the *Tyndall Register*, or at least it hadn't by the end of the year.

Perhaps later editions of the paper would have that news, but it was now nearing five o'clock and it was time for the library to close. Deciding that I'd done enough for one day, I saved my work and closed down my laptop. As the librarian began locking up for the evening, I said, "Would the library have any phone books or City Directories going back to the 1920s?"

"No, I'm sorry but we don't anymore. I suppose it's possible that the Heritage Museum might have something like that, but if so, I'm not aware of it."

"Do the last names Kratina or Sedlaceck mean anything to you?"

"You mean living around here?"

"Right."

She shook her head. "No, I don't think I've ever heard of anybody around here with those names. Sorry."

"One last question, does the library have a current history of South Dakota that I might borrow and look at overnight? I know I'm not a resident and I don't have a library card, but I promise to bring the book back tomorrow and I'd be happy to leave a cash deposit."

Smiling, she said, "I think we can probably trust you overnight. Just a minute."

She disappeared into the stacks for a moment and returned with a book titled *History of South Dakota*, by Herbert S. Schell. As she handed me the book, I thanked her again for her help and told her I'd be back the following afternoon to continue working through the newspapers.

12.

It was a bit early to be thinking about dinner, and so I decided to drop by the Dugout for the cocktail hour. When I walked through the door, Matt, the owner, greeted me like a long-lost friend and said, "MGD?"

"Perfect," I said, wandering over to look again at the pictures of my grandfather on the wall.

The place was a little busier than it had been on my first visit, and when I turned to sit down, I saw that the bartender had set my beer in front of a stool next to two women, a blonde and a brunette, both of whom appeared to be in their middle forties, and who were drinking some variety of white wine. I nodded at the women, slid the beer down the bar a bit, and took a seat leaving one stool between me and the brunette. She took a sip of wine, leaving a pronounced red lipstick mark on the glass, then set the glass on the bar and gave me a big smile. "You don't have to be unfriendly now, we don't bite!"

Her partner in crime leaned around and gave me what I what I gathered was supposed to be a conspiratorial smile. Then she winked and said, "Well, at least not in here, anyways."

At that point the bartender intervened to say, "Now, you girls need to be minding your own business and not harassing the other customers." Turning to me, he said, "How ya doin', Jack?"

I fluttered my hand. "So-so, Matt, and you?"

"Well, I could complain, but it wouldn't do any good, so I won't."

The brunette finished her wine and without asking, Matt reached into the cooler behind him, grabbed a bottle of Chablis, and filled her glass again. She took a fairly healthy sip and sighed as if she'd really needed it. Then she turned to me again. "So, you're Jack, the ghost's grandson."

"Well, as I told Matt here, I really don't believe in ghosts."

The woman's friend, who already appeared to be more than a little tipsy, shook her head, tossing her hair. "Well, I sure as hell do. I've *heard* that creepy guy walking around here at night in the dark."

The brunette snickered. "And we all know what you were doing here in the dark, don't we, Darlene? Girl, I'm amazed that you could hear anything, let alone some damned ghost."

Looking to the bartender, the blonde retorted, "Well, we did hear it, didn't we, Matt?"

The bartender colored a bit and then suddenly decided to wipe down the bar. Looking at the bar and not at the woman, he said, "Sure sounded like him to me."

* * *

Fifteen minutes later, the two women finished their drinks and said their goodbyes, along with a couple that had been sitting two stools down from them. A stocky guy at the end of the bar who appeared to be somewhere in his early fifties, watched them all out the door and then laughed. "The ghost that haunts the bar? Jesus Christ, Reingold, how long have you been running that gag, anyhow?"

The bartender shrugged and shook his head. Declining to answer the guy's question, he turned to me. "So, how's your research going, Jack?"

I drained the last of the beer. He grabbed another from the cooler, opened it and set it in front of me. "Okay, I guess. I'm not really learning anything that I didn't know before I got up here, but I am filling in some of the blanks, reading the old newspapers at the library."

The guy at the end of the bar was wearing jeans, work boots and a green shirt with the name "Mack" stitched into the pocket.

He had longish brown hair and dark eyes and looked like he'd just dropped in for a drink on his way home from work. He signaled Matt for another Budweiser and said, "So you're the guy whose grandfather damn near ruined this town."

Suddenly feeling the need to defend my grandfather's reputation, I said, "Well, that might be something of an exaggeration. I'm sure that what he did caused problems for a lot of people, but reading the papers from back then, and from what I've seen of the town over the last couple of days, the town was hardly ruined."

He took a long pull on his beer and said, "Oh yeah? You could try telling that to *my* grandfather if he were still around."

"How's that?"

"Back then, my granddad owned the farm implement company here in town. He had his savings in this fuckin' bank and so did a lot of the poor bastards who'd bought tractors and other farm equipment on credit from him. When the bank went under after your grandfather helped himself to their money, the farmers couldn't get their money out of the bank to pay my grandfather, and he couldn't get *his* money out of the bank to pay the manufacturers who had sold him equipment on credit.

"My grandfather wound up on the verge of bankruptcy and had to sell out, which meant that my father, instead of inheriting the business, wound up working as a mechanic for the Bensons. And it meant that instead of me inheriting the business from him and being my own man, I wound up working as a damned heating and air conditioning repair man, living from paycheck to paycheck, while another family is making a goddamned fortune out of the company that my grandfather started. And it all goes back to that old man ruining this bank and a lot of peoples' lives along with it. And so, yeah, I'm still pissed, and I'm sure I'm not the only one."

"Well, it's not going to do any good to say that I'm sorry, but I am."

"You're right; it's not going to do any good. I heard that you were in town, digging all this up again, and I just wanted to get a look at you. Now I have, and I've said my piece."

With that, the guy drained the last of his beer, dropped a bill on the bar, and walked out the door without saying anything more, leaving the place temporarily empty, save for the bartender and me. Matt watched him go and shook his head. "Don't pay any attention to that asshole, Jack. The guy's never amounted to anything, mostly because he's too damned lazy to make anything of himself. For as long as I've known him, he's always been blaming other people for his problems and your granddad is only one in a long line of people that he thinks screwed him over."

"Should I worry about him?"

"Naw. Mack's one of those guys who talks like a big man but who never backs it up. He's all hat and no cattle."

"So, I said, "he brought up the Benson company. What's the general feeling around here about them?"

Looking a bit surprised, he said, "Why are you asking about them?"

I waved off the question. "Just curious. George Benson was the head cashier at the bank when my grandfather worked there. After the bank failed, Benson went to work for the guy who originally owned the farm implement business—apparently that guy's grandfather. Then, three years later, he bought the guy out and renamed the business for himself."

"Well, the company's been there, right where it is, all my life. As far as I know, people are happy doing business with them, and I guess they must be for as long as they've lasted around here."

"What about the Bensons themselves?"

"Old man Benson—that is the guy *I* think of as old man Benson, the father of the current owner—was a rock-solid kind of guy who'd go out of his way to do a favor for anybody, whether they were a customer of his or not. As far as I know, everybody

68

really liked him. He died nine or ten years ago, and his son, Alex, is in charge now."

Even though we were the only two people in the bar at the moment, he leaned over and dropped his voice to a whisper. "Truth to tell, Alex has always been something of an arrogant little prick, but as I understand it, he pretty much leaves things over there in the hands of his general manager. The G.M. is a decent guy and so, at least as far as I know, they're still doing well."

"Is there anybody left around who might remember the older Bensons—if not George, then maybe his son, George, Junior?"

He scrunched his forehead up in thought, then shook his head. "Nobody that I can think of off the top of my head."

"Does the name Ted Grimke mean anything to you?"

"I remember a girl named Sarah Grimke. She was several years ahead of me, but as I recall, her dad's name was John."

"If Ted Grimke was a couple of generations back, maybe he could have been her grandfather?"

"Maybe."

"Does Sarah Grimke still live around here?"

"Yeah, she's Sarah Paine now. She runs the hardware store a couple of blocks down the street with her husband, Dennis."

At that moment, the door pushed open and two couples walked through and took a table near the bar. Matt filled four glasses with water, grabbed some menus, and walked over to greet them. Figuring that I'd accomplished about as much as I was going to in here for the evening, I drained the last of my beer, dropped a twenty on the bar and said goodnight to Matt on my way out the door.

13.

It was now six thirty, and I decided it was time for dinner. I went back up to the café and took the same booth I'd had last night. The young waitress came over to serve me and, on her recommendation, I had a pork chop with oven-browned potatoes, followed by a piece of cherry pie. Nobody came by to bitch at me about my grandfather having ruined the town, and so I took my time, eating slowly and thoroughly enjoying the food.

After dinner, I drifted back on down to the Welcome Inn and spent twenty minutes on the phone with Annie, catching her up on my research to date. She told me about her week at the hospital thus far and said, "You're still planning on being back on Saturday, aren't you, Jack?"

"I am. And if you don't have another hot date already lined up, why don't you let me take you to Eddie V's for dinner? Al Ortiz is playing in the lounge that night."

"Well, I have had three or four other offers for the weekend, but I've put them all on hold until I knew for sure what your plans were. Now that I know you're going to be back I'll tell those other guys that I'm going to be busy all the way through the weekend."

She paused for a moment, then lowered her voice. "I *am* going to be busy all the way through the weekend, aren't I?"

"*Very* busy, I promise. I know I've only been gone for a couple of days, but I'm really missing you."

"I'm missing you too, Jack, more than you probably know, and I'll really be looking forward to Saturday night."

"I will too, Annie, and I'll call you again in a day or two."

* * *

By the time I was through talking to Annie, it was still only a little after eight. Feeling restless and a bit at loose ends, I decided to go for a walk. Speculating that my computer would probably be safer in the car than in the motel room, I locked it in the trunk and headed up the street. I spent an hour or so walking along the streets of the little town, thinking about my grandfather and again wondering what might have caused him to violate the trust that his community had placed in him and what he might have done with the money he had stolen.

To all outward appearances, he led a simple life and had not been spending money extravagantly. Given the tone of the article about his funeral, it appeared that virtually everyone regarded him as an upstanding member of the community, and even when the fraud was discovered, the newspaper's editor had simply reported the plain facts of the matter without openly revising his earlier estimate of my grandfather's character.

There was also no discussion in the paper about what might have happened to the money, and I found that more than a little odd. Given that the money had effectively been stolen out of the pockets of many of Tyndall's citizens, I would have thought that its whereabouts would have been a principal topic of discussion around the town. And perhaps it had been in the bars and cafes, and at the feed store and other such places where the bank's depositors gathered to discuss the news of the day. But if so, the discussion never made it into the pages of the local paper.

I assumed that if my grandfather had used the money for some speculative venture—to invest in the stock market or in real estate or whatever, there would have been some record of the investments and perhaps at least some of the money could have been recovered. But that seemed clearly not to be the case. Perhaps he'd had a serious gambling problem, but I found it hard to imagine that anyone could have lost nearly two hundred thousand dollars playing poker or whatever in the Bon Homme County of the 1920s without a lot of people knowing about it.

I arrived back at the motel no wiser than I had been upon leaving for my walk, so I decided to forget about the whole business for the rest of the night and climbed back into bed with Schell's *History of South Dakota.* I flipped to a chapter titled, "The Twenties and Thirties—Hard Times and the New Deal," and discovered that, state-wide, the economic crisis was even worse than I had gathered by reading the Tyndall papers.

As the agricultural depression gathered momentum in the early Twenties, declining farm income and property values had made it difficult, if not impossible, for many farmers to meet their obligations to the banks. According to Schell, over one hundred and seventy-five banks had already failed in the state even before the Security Bank of Tyndall went under in 1925. State efforts to relieve the crisis were increasingly ineffective, and hard times were well under way in South Dakota by the time the Depression spread from the agricultural heartland to the nation as a whole.

The banking crisis had huge implications for the state's budget overall, and amidst charges that the State Banking Department had mismanaged the growing problem, Fred R. Smith, the Superintendent of Banks who had been responsible for overseeing the liquidation of the Security Bank, was arrested after he confessed to embezzling $1,200,000 from the assets of the closed state banks he was administering. If all that weren't bad enough, drought, crop failures, severe winter weather and a grasshopper infestation further hammered the state. During the 1920s over 30,000 farm foreclosures were instituted in South Dakota, and the number began to rise sharply in the Thirties. Between 1920 and 1934, seventy-one percent of the banks in the state had failed, costing depositors around $39 million.

By 1933, the situation had grown truly critical and some farmers and other South Dakotans turned to radical action to address their problems, though movements like the Farm Holiday Association, which attempted to raise farm prices by withholding crops from the market. Things would finally begin to improve with the advent of the New Deal's relief and other programs, particularly those like the Agricultural Adjustment Act, the Soil Conservation and Domestic Allotment Act, and others aimed at the agricultural sector. Through the Thirties, large numbers of farmers and other South Dakotans depended upon the programs of the federal government for their very survival. Fortunately, though, as a result of those programs and other factors, the nation's economy finally began to improve, and while the recovery was not complete by the end of the Thirties, the crisis of the Great Depression had largely passed.

I closed the book with a better understanding of the general context of the situation in Tyndall and feeling a great deal of sympathy for my grandmother and her family and for all the other poor souls who had suffered the misfortune of living through this very difficult period in our nation's history. I was still pondering the seeming unfairness in all of this when I finally fell into a deep sleep.

14.

The next morning, I dropped by the café long enough to grab a cup of coffee and then drove a couple of blocks down the street to the hardware store. It turned out to be a fairly old-fashioned business, individually owned and operated—the kind of hardware store you would have found in any small town before the Lowes and the Home Depots and all the other big box stores rendered so many of them unprofitable and irrelevant. The place even smelled like an old-fashioned hardware store and seemed to have in stock a little bit of everything from kitchen appliances to plumbing supplies to lawn and garden tools, to paint, and pretty much everything in between.

A tall thin woman who looked to be in her early sixties was standing behind the counter wearing a red apron with the name "Sarah" embroidered above her left breast. She had longish gray hair that was tied back into a ponytail and lively blue eyes. She smiled as I approached the counter and said, "Good morning. Can I help you?"

"I hope so, but I'm not sure. My name is Jack Oliva and my family lived here in the 1920s. I'm up here doing some research into my family's history and came across the name Ted Grimke. Matt, up at the Dugout, suggested that he might have been your grandfather and pointed me in your direction."

She nodded. "Well, he's right; Ted Grimke was my grandfather. Are we related somehow?"

"No. The connection I'm pursuing at the moment is a pretty tenuous one, but my grandfather and George Benson, the man who founded the farm implement company, worked together back in the Twenties before Benson founded the implement company in 1928. According to the state records, your grandfather was a minor stockholder in the company and served on the original board of directors.

"I'm assuming, of course, that your grandfather would no longer be living, but I was just wondering if your father or mother might still be alive and if so, if I might be able talk to them to see if they had any memories of those people."

Again, she smiled. "Well, my mom died about ten years ago, but my dad is still alive, and he's a man with a lot of stories. Coincidentally, he was born in 1928, which I gather from what you just said, is the same year that my grandfather joined the Benson company. I've never heard Dad talk about any of that but that isn't to say that he doesn't know anything about it."

"Does your father still live here in town?"

She nodded. "He's ninety-one now and lives out at the Prairie View Assisted Living Center. He's got some physical problems and so he can't live on his own anymore, but he's still sharp as a tack mentally."

"Do you think he'd mind having a visitor?"

She laughed. "The better question is, would you mind having your ear talked off for the best part of an afternoon? Once Dad gets wound up, it's pretty hard to shut him down."

"Well, I'd certainly enjoy the opportunity to talk with him. Are there scheduled visiting hours, or can you just drop in at any time?"

She looked at her watch. "If you went directly out there now, it would probably be your best bet. You'd get there a little after ten and they take Dad down to lunch at noon, which would give you an excellent opportunity to make your escape. Otherwise, today being Thursday, he doesn't have physical therapy or anything else regularly scheduled in the afternoon. If you go out there after lunch, you could find yourself trapped until he goes to dinner at five thirty."

* * *

I thanked the woman for her help, and she offered to call her father to tell him that I'd be coming. She gave me directions to the assisted living facility, which was on the north end of town, and I fired up the Chrysler and headed in that direction.

The place turned out to be a rambling, one-story brick structure with a porte-cochere in front. It looked and smelled like every other nursing home I'd ever visited, and walking through the front door, I was again hugely grateful for the fact that I'd filed an Advance Health Care Directive with the state of Arizona which provided, effectively, that if the day ever came when I needed to be moved into such a place, I should simply be left alone in a room for fifteen or twenty minutes with my service revolver close at hand.

A woman in an actual nurse's outfit—the starched, white uniform that nurses had routinely worn until sometime in the 1970s—was sitting behind the reception desk. I told her that I was there to visit John Grimke and she had me sign a guest register. She then hailed a young woman who appeared to be an orderly of some sort and asked her to show me to Grimke's room.

I followed the woman down a couple of hallways and then stopped as she knocked on a door that was slightly ajar. "Mr. Grimke?" she asked. "Someone here to see you."

A voice from inside the room said, "Come on in, Honey," and she pushed the door open and peeked into the room. "Just wanted to make sure you were decent, before we came barging in."

She led me into a medium-sized room with pale gray walls, which was configured for a single resident. A regulation hospital bed with the rails down was situated in the middle of the room with the headboard butting up against the long wall of the room. The rest of the furniture, including a dresser, a couple of tables and three chairs, looked like it had been moved into the room from someone's home—Grimke's, I assumed. A flat-screen TV sat on a long narrow table opposite the bed and next to the window, a frail-looking man with a few strands of wispy white hair sat in a recliner.

He could have been anywhere from eighty-five to ninety-five; there gets to be a point when you can't really tell with older people and where it really doesn't matter all that much anyhow. Neatly dressed in a golf shirt, chinos, and a pair of boat shoes, he had piercing blue eyes, much like his daughter, and something of a mischievous look that, at first glance, confirmed her observation that, while physically weakened, the guy was still very alert mentally. He had a hardback book in his lap, and as we walked into the room, he stuck a bookmark in it to save his place and then set the book on a table beside the chair. Looking up at me he said, "You're the guy Sarah just called about?"

I approached the chair and stuck out my hand. "Yes, I am, sir. Jack Oliva."

"John Grimke," he replied shaking my hand with what was still a fairly strong grip.

The young orderly interrupted to say, "Well, I'll leave you two to your conversation."

I thanked for her leading me to the room and Grimke directed me to a chair on the other side of the table. "What are you reading?" I asked.

"John Sandford's new Lucas Davenport novel."

"There's a coincidence; I'm reading Sandford's previous book now—the Virgil Flowers novel."

He laughed. "Oh yeah; that's a good one. I love that Fuckin' Flowers."

"I haven't met anyone yet who doesn't. Do you read a lot of crime fiction?"

"Yup, always have. I've got hundreds of the damned books at home. Sarah occasionally picks up a new one for me and rotates through some of the ones from the house so that I've always got a few here. I much prefer reading to watching most of the crap that you see on television, and truth to tell, most days I'd much rather just sit here in my room with a good book as opposed to hanging around in the common rooms with all the old farts who live here. I don't mind telling you, that can get pretty damned depressing."

"I can certainly understand that."

"So, you look like a retired guy yourself, Jack. What did you used to do?"

"I was a homicide detective down in Phoenix."

Grimke's face brightened. "The hell you say. Just like Lucas."

I laughed. "Not at all like Lucas, I'm afraid. Reading about most of my cases would have put a person soundly to sleep before they got to the third page."

"So, you never had to shoot anybody?"

Nodding in the direction of the book he'd been reading, I said, "A couple of times over a career that spanned the better part of thirty-five years. Certainly not a couple of times a week, like old Lucas there."

That got a laugh. "My daughter tells me that you're up here doing research into your family."

"That's right. My family lived up here for about thirty years. My mom was born here in 1919, and my grandfather, whose name was Charles Kratina, died here in 1925. My grandmother then moved the family to Montana in the middle 1930s. Anyhow, I'm just trying to get an idea of what their life was like when they were living in Tyndall."

Grimke nodded. "I remember when I was a kid, hearing stories about your grandad shooting himself in the bank. That must have been a helluva thing for your mother and grandmother."

"I imagine that it was, but the strange thing is, I never knew anything about it at all until just a few weeks ago. My mother and grandmother never talked about my grandpa and when I asked, my mother told me that he'd been killed in a bank robbery. After she died, I found a picture of him that she'd stuck away in a box and I started to do some research on the Internet. That's when I discovered that he'd stolen money from the bank and then killed himself. I got intrigued by the story and so I decided to come up here to dig into it a little bit, but mostly just to get a feel for the place."

"So, what did you want to talk to me about?"

"Well, as I told your daughter, this is a pretty nebulous connection, but looking into all of this, I became curious about George Benson, the guy who founded the farm implement company here in 1928. He and my grandfather had worked together at the bank before the bank failed. I discovered that your father had been a minor stockholder in Benson's company and had served on the company's board of directors. I was wondering if you remembered anything that your father might have said about the company or about Benson himself."

He nodded. "My dad was Benson's lawyer. Benson gave him a few shares of stock in the company as compensation for the legal services Dad performed for him. The arrangement continued until my dad died and then I inherited both the shares in the company and the seat on the board of directors.

"By then, I was already doing most of their legal work, and I continued to be the company's attorney until I retired. At that point, they hired a new firm to take over the legal work and my seat on the board went to Tom Benson's brother, Bill. It turned out to be a pretty good deal for both my dad and me, because the dividends from the stock more than covered what we would have normally charged them for the work we were doing for them."

"I'm curious about how George Benson wound up in the farm implement business. It seems an odd transition to move from being a banker to selling tractors."

Grimke took a sip from a glass of water on the table next to him. "Maybe not all that odd, given the times and the circumstances. This is a very small town, and it wasn't all that much bigger back then. When the bank failed, I would imagine that there weren't that many opportunities for Benson in the banking industry unless he wanted to pull up stakes and move someplace else. Even then, banks were failing right and left, and I'd imagine that jobs were hard to find, even if you did have a lot of experience and very good references. And, of course, I'd imagine that Benson's references wouldn't have been all that great, given that he failed to report the fraud that destroyed the bank he was working for.

"I knew the guy when I was growing up, especially since my dad handled his legal work, and I have to tell you, he was a shrewd businessman and a natural-born salesman if there ever was one. I'm sure that he was right in his element selling farm equipment, even in the middle of a depression. And when the opportunity to buy the business presented itself, he decided to take advantage of it."

"I would think that must have been a pretty risky investment at that point."

Grimke shrugged. "Back then of course, practically any investment was risky. But the smart money saw an opportunity to buy low and profit down the road a bit. I'd assume that was Benson's thinking."

"I'd have no idea what he might have paid for the business, but I'd assume he would have needed a fair amount of capital to buy it and then nurse it through the Depression until farmers could afford to buy equipment again. Do you have any idea where he got the money?"

"The lucky bastard inherited it. Just when the economy was going down the tubes and most folks were struggling to make ends meet, Benson's uncle died back east somewhere. The guy had no kids and George was his only close relative, so he inherited the estate. He had the uncle's lawyer cash everything out and then he used the money to buy the business and position himself to become the biggest farm implement dealer in three or four counties once the hard times had passed. The rest, as they say, is history."

"What were your impressions of the guy when you were growing up?"

"As a kid, I remember him as a nice guy, quick with a funny story. George Senior and his wife were close friends of my parents and so they occasionally came over to our house for dinner. The two families sometimes got together for a picnic or some such thing. Benson genuinely liked children and was always quick to sneak you a piece of candy out of his pocket when he thought your parents weren't looking.

"Later, I also came to understand that he'd been very astute during the Depression, definitely playing the long game, if you know what I mean. The way the farm implement business worked back then was that the manufacturers provided tractors and other such goods to the dealers on credit. The dealers then sold them on credit to farmers. Either that, or the manufacturing company itself advanced the credit to the farmers through the dealers. Theoretically, the farmers made their payments on time and everything was copacetic, as the kids used to say.

"Of course, in the 1920s and '30s, things didn't work nearly that smoothly. Often, the farmers simply couldn't make their payments to the dealers on time and so the dealer either had to repossess the equipment and try to sell it or otherwise carry the farmer on their books while somehow paying their own obligations to the manufacturers. Of course, sometimes the dealers couldn't make their payments to the manufacturers or to the banks or whomever, and they wound up going out of business.

And that's basically how George Senior wound up buying the company in the first place."

"I understood that something like that had happened."

The old man nodded. "Through the Thirties, George was extremely lenient with farmers who were struggling and who couldn't meet their obligations to him. I gather that he had enough of a cushion built up to keep the banks and the manufacturers somewhat happy, but he created a lot of good will for the company back then and it paid dividends for years to come."

"I understand that his son, George Junior, took over when he died. What were your impressions of him?"

"Well, it was only a few years after he took over the company that I went into practice with my father and started assisting with their legal business. Ultimately, I became Junior's personal attorney as well as doing work for the firm. Again, a very nice guy and very fair. Somewhat shy and introspective. Not the natural salesman that his father was, but probably smarter than his dad. Junior ran the company for the better part of thirty years, and working off the foundation his father established, he expanded the business significantly."

"And then?"

"Junior retired in '75, and George's grandson, Tom, took over. I worked with him until I retired in 2001. He hung on until he died of a heart attack in 2009, and then the dealership went to his son, Alex. Tom was basically a caretaker, not nearly as bright or as motivated as either his grandfather or his father. The business continued to do very well, but then by the time Junior retired, it was pretty much running on autopilot. A person would have had to be especially stupid to screw it up by that point."

"And Alex?"

He snorted. "There's the kid who might actually be stupid enough to fuck the whole thing up, if you'll excuse my French. He started working for the company when he finished college in the early nineties and so had about fifteen years under his belt there when his dad died. Fortunately, I never had to work with him, and I don't really know him all that well. But he's obviously not all that interested in the business itself and he's basically using the company as a cash cow.

"He married this snotty woman from Los Angeles, I believe, and both of them think they're much too sophisticated to be living out here in the sticks. From what little I hear, I understand that they're living large—if not way beyond their means, then close to it. I'm sure you know the old adage about rich families going from shirtsleeves to shirtsleeves in three generations? Well, I'm thinking that in this case it could well be four."

I nodded my thanks, "All of that is very useful, Mr. Grimke. Let me shift gears on you here. You were born in 1928, which means that you were here for at least a few years before my grandmother moved her family to Montana. Do you have any memories of them?"

"I vaguely remember Dick Kratina, who was the youngest kid in the family and who was about five years older than I. I had the sense that the family was constantly struggling. As a practical matter, there weren't really enough people living in Tyndall at that time to have significant class divisions, but clearly some people were doing better than others. And I'm sorry to say that after your grandfather killed himself, his family would have been among the poorer families in town.

"I do have a very dim recollection of your grandmother as being something of a heavyset woman. I think she did laundry for some of the other families in town, at least for a while, and it's possible that she might even have done my family's laundry for a brief period when I was very young. But other than that, I really don't remember her."

"Do you remember whether there was any lingering animosity toward her and her family because of what my grandfather had done?"

"Not that I noticed, but then again, I was still very young when they finally left Tyndall, and so there could have been a lot of things going on that I wasn't really aware of. I have the sense that a lot of people around here felt sorry for your grandmother and realized that she wasn't really to blame for what your grandfather had done. If she had suddenly started living way above her apparent means, I'm sure it would have been a different story, but clearly, that wasn't the case. And when you get right down to it, nobody was more adversely affected by what your grandfather did than she was."

"After my grandmother moved to Montana, were there any Kratinas left in the area?"

He shook his head. "I don't believe so. I think there were one or two other families by that name who were living here around that time, but they must have died or moved before your grandmother left. I'm sure there weren't any others here after that."

"What about Sedlacecks? That was my grandmother's maiden name."

"I went to grade school with a couple of cousins named Sedlaceck. But the two families pulled up and left together in the late 1930s. Went to California, I think, and they were the last families here by that name."

* * *

We visited for another ten minutes or so before the orderly who had led me to the room appeared again, saying that it was time to take Grimke down to lunch. I expressed my appreciation for all his help, and he encouraged me to stop by again if I had the time before leaving town. "I'd love to hear some of your stories about being a detective," he said.

"I will if I get a chance. In the meantime, I need to get some lunch myself and then head on back to the library."

15.

Back at the café, I fortified myself with an excellent turkey sandwich and a piece of strawberry-rhubarb pie. On the basis of two experiments, I would have said that the young waitress from my first night in town was not exaggerating; if her aunt didn't make the best pies in the state, I couldn't imagine who would.

A little after one o'clock, I was back in the library ready to resume my research. Anticipating my arrival, the librarian had loaded the *Tyndall Register* into the microfilm reader, and I wound through the spool to the beginning of 1926. I was just opening my laptop, getting ready to take notes, when the librarian came over to the table with an envelope in her hand. "I found this wedged in the front door when I came to open this afternoon," she said, "and I'm assuming it must be intended for you."

It was a plain white number ten envelope, the kind you might buy in any store that sold office or school supplies. Typed on the front of the envelope were the words, "FOR THE RESEARCHER."

I took the envelope, turned it over, but saw nothing else to indicate where the envelope might have come from or who might have sent it. I looked up to the librarian. "You're sure this is intended for me?"

"Well, you're the only one who's done any research in here over the last couple of weeks. I can't imagine who else it might be for."

"Okay then, why don't we open it?"

I took a small penknife from my computer bag—one that I'd forgotten about and that the TSA had missed on my way through the airport—and slit open the envelope. A sheet of paper had been folded into thirds and placed in the envelope, and I set the envelope on the table and gently worked the paper out with the penknife. Using a tissue and the knife, I unfolded the paper on the table, careful not to touch it. The message on the sheet was direct and to the point:

YOU SHOULDN'T BE POKING YOUR NOSE INTO THINGS THAT DON'T CONCERN YOU.

IF YOU KNOW WHAT'S GOOD FOR YOU, YOU WILL PACK UP AND LEAVE RIGHT NOW.

THIS IS THE ONLY WARNING YOU WILL GET!!!

Reading the note over my shoulder, the librarian brought a hand to her mouth and said, "Oh, my goodness!"

"Indeed. Who do you suppose I've antagonized by reading some old newspapers?"

"I can't imagine. What are you going to do?"

"Well, I think I'd better carefully preserve this note and then I'm going to get back to work. Would you have a plastic bag or something like that I could use?"

While the librarian returned to her desk, I used the tissue to carefully refold the letter and put it back into the envelope. The librarian came back with a thin plastic envelope and I slid my envelope into hers. The woman was obviously unsettled by the experience and said, "Do you think we should call the sheriff?"

"I don't think we need to do that, at least not at the moment, but perhaps you might hold onto this envelope and put it in your desk or someplace safe, just on the off chance that something might happen to me. *Then* you can give it to the sheriff."

That seemed to unnerve her even more and so I said, "Look, I really wouldn't worry about this. It's probably just someone playing an odd joke, and even if it isn't, I can't imagine that anyone seriously intends to do me any kind of harm, and certainly not while I'm here in the library."

"Well, I'm not really worried that someone might attack you in here, but I don't like the thought that someone might attack you somewhere else either. Tyndall just isn't the kind of town where that sort of thing would happen."

"Well, judging by what I've seen of the town so far, I'd certainly agree with your assessment. And, frankly, I'm curious about the letter and about why someone would want to warn me away from this project. But I'm not really frightened by it. In my experience, people who send anonymous threats are the sorts of people who generally aren't brave enough to follow through on them."

"I certainly hope not, but I also hope that you'll be careful."

I promised her that I would be on guard, and at that point another customer came into the library and walked up to the front desk. The librarian moved over to assist the woman and I sat there for a moment wondering who might have been angered or might have felt threatened by my research. More to the point, who even knew that I was in town doing research in the first place?

I'd barely been in town for forty-eight hours and outside of Mack, the guy at the Dugout last night, no one had seemed even mildly annoyed either by my presence in town or by my research into my family's history in Tyndall. Who could possibly be upset about it? I turned the problem over in my mind for a few minutes but, coming up with no plausible answers, I returned to the papers for 1926.

The first major local news of the year occurred the second week in January. A banner headline in the *Tyndall Register* for January 13, announced, "Sheriff Dies in Apparent Hunting Accident."

The story went on to say that Hal Howard, the county sheriff, had been found shot to death in a wooded area fourteen miles outside of Tyndall. The sheriff had been hunting deer alone, and his own weapon had not been fired. He had apparently been wearing clothing that more or less blended in with the woods around him. A group of three other hunters had found the body, but no one had come forward to take responsibility for firing the shot that had killed the sheriff.

The investigation into the incident was headed by Gary Checka, the sheriff's principal deputy, but there was apparently little evidence to be found. It appeared that the victim had been shot from some distance away, and the deputy sheriff speculated that the person who fired the fatal shot might not even have been aware of the fact that it had struck another hunter. The deputy was attempting to identify anyone else who might have been hunting in the general area on that day and asked anyone who might have any information about the incident to please come forward.

Through the next several editions of the paper, the mystery remained unresolved. A large crowd attended the sheriff's funeral and he was given a burial with full honors. A memorial fund had been established for his wife and three children, and the county commissioners had appointed Deputy Checka to serve as interim sheriff until the next election. Then, two weeks after the funeral, the newspaper reported that, "Mystery Surrounds Former Sheriff."

According to the article, in settling the affairs of the former sheriff, his safe deposit box at the First National Bank had been opened in the presence of his wife, a bank officer, and the county attorney, apparently as prescribed by law. Much to the surprise of everyone, apparently including the wife, the contents of the box included $8700 in cash. The sheriff's salary was less than a thousand dollars a year, and no one could explain where the money might have come from. Even though there was no evidence to suggest that the sheriff might not have come by the money honestly, the county attorney took possession of the cash, pending an investigation.

Two months later, the paper reported that the money had been given to the sheriff's widow as part of his estate. The investigation into the matter, involving both the county attorney and the sheriff's office, failed to provide any explanation for how the sheriff might have acquired the money, but there was nothing to suggest that he had done so illegally.

The paper noted that the sheriff had always had an impeccable reputation both as a lawman and as a citizen of the community and that the matter was likely to remain a mystery. The sheriff's widow noted that her late husband's father had lost all of his savings in a bank failure years earlier and that, as a result, her husband had never trusted banks. She added that her husband had always been a very frugal man and suggested that the money found in his safe deposit box probably represented the savings that he had slowly accumulated over a long life of hard work. And there the matter seemed to rest.

* * *

Meanwhile, in late January, the paper had articles about two other banks in neighboring towns that had failed, including the bank at Kingsburg. The paper reported that the cashier, Mr. Pier, had "made a desperate fight against circumstances and conditions in an effort to keep the bank running and no doubt would have succeeded except for the almost complete corn crop failure in that section last year which made it impossible for borrowers to meet their obligations."

Reading the story made me wonder how strong the Security Bank would have been had it not been for my grandfather's thefts. I assumed that most of the bank's assets were tied up in mortgages and other loans that it had made to farmers in the surrounding countryside. Given the depressed conditions and the fact that farmers and others were clearly having difficulty meeting their obligations to the banks, would the Security Bank have been able to survive even without the thefts?

Early in February 1926, the paper published a brief story noting that the state banking department had dispatched checks for a ten percent dividend to the creditors of the Security Bank. The total monies expended in the payout amounted to $60,400. The depositors also received Certificates of Indebtedness for the other ninety percent of the money owed them. The certificates would bear an interest rate of five percent and were negotiable. So, roughly nine months after the bank had failed, the depositors finally got a tiny percentage of their money back, with the promise of more to come. But I wondered how much would they actually get in the long run, and how many of them would be forced to part with their certificates almost immediately for pennies on the dollar in an effort to meet their current expenses?

As if to answer my question, on March fourth, the *Register* published a letter from the administrators, regarding "The Condition of Security Bank." They reported that, where possible, the bank had continued to collect payments due on the loans it had made. In other cases, it had foreclosed on properties when the payments were not made. The bank was attempting to sell these properties and would use the proceeds to repay its creditors. "Final collection of the money from which to pay dividends to creditors from such items depends upon the ability to sell the real estate in which the bank is interested. Many of the loans carried by the bank were secured by real estate mortgages which have been foreclosed and the lands described in such mortgages are now held by the bank under Sheriff's Certificates of sale."

The report insisted that those responsible for the bank's liquidation were doing the very best they could under very difficult conditions and that they were undeserving of the "unwarranted and too often unjust criticism" that had been directed against them." The report insisted that the Examiner in Charge and the Department of Banking intended to pay dividends to the depositors "whenever sufficient funds are on hand to pay a ten percent dividend."

The report concluded, noting that "a good crop during the coming year and good prices for the crop will make a tremendous difference in the amount of liquidation to be secured in this bank.... The depositors are urged to use their best influence with the debtors of the bank to persuade them to realize the obligation they have. Payment to the depositors depends entirely upon the payment of obligations due the bank by its debtors. When a debtor fails to pay a closed bank, he is not depriving the Examiner in Charge or the Department of Banking of any particular benefit. He is, on the other hand, depriving his neighbors and friends whose money was loaned to him by the bank, of the opportunity to secure the return of the funds to which they are justly entitled."

It was hard not to sympathize with the bank's directors and others who were attempting to liquidate the bank's assets and to repay the creditors as quickly as possible, and I could imagine that there had been a lot of criticism of their efforts by depositors who were increasingly desperate to get their money back. I had no idea what the harvest might have been like in 1926, but given the circumstances, it was hard to imagine that, even in the case of a good harvest farm prices would suddenly rise dramatically, enabling farmers to dig themselves out of the hole and repay their mortgages.

I assumed that the depositors of the Security Bank and other failed institutions were in for a long haul, and indicative of the continuing problems, on June 17, the paper reported that a local farmer, about thirty-five years old, had shot himself to death the previous evening, leaving a wife and two children. "Despondency over financial affairs and temporary mental derangement are given as likely causes for the action."

Skimming through the rest of the papers for 1926, I found nothing much of interest, save for the fact that in August, state banking officials paid another ten percent dividend to the depositors of the Security Bank. Prohibition was still in effect in 1926, of course, and on July 2, the paper noted that the Beringer Pool Hall was closed by state marshals after several witnesses before Judge Elliott "swore they had drunk liquor in there a number of times."

Meanwhile, Bebe Daniels was back at the Cozy Theatre, starring in "Wild, Wild Susan." According to the ad, "Susan was a slave to thrills with a kick. And when she went out into the world to get them, she got them and then some!" Also on the bill was "Too Many Kisses," with Richard Dix, who "just couldn't make his lips behave!"

Not surprisingly, I supposed, the paper was apparently still having problems collecting from subscribers and in late October, the editor reported that an old criminal had once been asked what was the first step that had led him to ruin. The man responded by saying that "The first thing that led to my downfall was cheating the editor out of two years' subscription. Once I did that, the devil got such a grip on me that I couldn't shake him off."

The paper did not have a sports page as such, but in December, it reported that the Lake Andes girls had driven to Tyndall for a game. Sadly, "the Tyndall girls did not display the pep, nor work as hard as they did in the Yankton game," and, as a consequence, they lost to Lake Andes, 88-4.

On that sad note, I saved my work a little before five o'clock, closed down the computer and said goodnight to the librarian. I'd earlier noticed a small flower shop on Main Street, and on the way back to the Welcome Inn, I stopped in and bought a mixed bouquet of flowers in a nice vase. Back at the motel, I took a long, refreshing shower before heading out to dinner at my new-found cousin's farm.

16.

Fifteen minutes before six o'clock, I got into the Chrysler, cranked the AC to "Max," and headed out of town. The route toward Bud's farm took me north up Willow Avenue, past the Czech National Cemetery which I spotted on the east side of the road. As the cemetery faded away behind me, I was once again in the heart of Serious Farm Country. Corn and soybeans appeared to be the principal crops in this part of the county, although I did spy an occasional wheat field. A number of farmers were also raising cattle and hogs, and passing some of these operations with the wind blowing in the right direction, I caught a very strong scent in the air that would have been totally foreign to the folks back home in Phoenix.

My cousin's directions were excellent, and promptly at six o'clock, I spotted his name on a mailbox and turned onto a long gravel road that led through a corn field and up to the house. While the farmhouses I had passed along the way had all seemed fairly modest, the Daniels home was anything but. It was a very large and impressive two-story brick home with a front porch that ran the length of the of the house.

A large red barn sat perhaps a hundred yards to the right of the house and appeared to be just as imposing. The buildings and the entire farm, for that matter, looked to be immaculately maintained, and my first impression was that my cousin was a man with a strong work ethic and perhaps an even stronger sense of pride in his operation.

As I pulled to a stop twenty yards from the house, a yellow lab came racing around the side of the house to greet me. Without making a sound, he skidded to a halt a few feet away from the car and sat down, panting and looking at me expectantly. I got out of the car, retrieved the flowers, and then approached the dog with my left arm out and my hand turned down. He sniffed at me for a few seconds and then, apparently deciding that I was sufficiently trustworthy, began licking my hand. At that moment, Bud Daniels came out of the house, holding a beer in his hand and shaking his head. "Be careful there, Jack. Cody could suddenly decide to rip your arm off."

I returned the laugh and headed for the steps up to the porch with Cody trailing behind me. Bud and I shook hands, and I said, "Yeah, he looks pretty ferocious all right. I don't imagine that you have to worry about much around here with him standing guard over the place."

"That's for damn sure," he said sarcastically, patting the dog on the head. "Some clown could back a United moving van up to the house while we're away and start robbing us blind. Then, after about three hours or so, Cody might finally butt them in the leg or something, looking for a snack."

The dog settled down on the porch, and Bud said, "Come on in and meet my wife."

Inside the front door was an entryway about twelve feet square, with louvered doors on the left that I assumed opened to a closet. A stairway on the right led up to a second floor that seemed to consist of two separate areas tied together by a bridge. Straight ahead was a bright, airy living room with a sloped ceiling that was probably eighteen or twenty feet high at its peak. The room looked to be professionally decorated with some interesting artwork and with furniture that suggested that this was the "formal" living room, which didn't actually get all that much use. Tall windows along the far wall looked across a large patio to the farm fields beyond.

Bud led me down a short hallway to the left into a big, well-equipped kitchen. The kitchen, in turn, opened into a family room with bookshelves, a large flat-screen TV and comfortable furniture. Clearly, this was the household's usual gathering spot.

A tall, handsome woman stood near the stove, stirring something in a medium-sized pan. She struck me as being somewhere around Annie's age, which would have put her in her early fifties, but like Annie, the years had treated her well. Long brown hair fell to her shoulder blades, streaked with a little grey here and there, but my immediate impression was that this was the sort of woman who would wear her age comfortably and not be all that concerned about the grey hair creeping in. She wore a pair of jeans and a blue and white striped shirt with the sleeves rolled up and the tails hanging out over the jeans. She looked up as Bud led me into the room, offered a big smile and said, "You must be Cousin Jack."

She turned the heat down under the pan, walked over and offered her hand. "I'm Becky."

"Jack," I replied, shaking her hand. "Something smells fantastic in here."

"Nothing too fancy, I'm afraid; it's Meatloaf Night."

"Obviously, then, Bud invited me out on the right night. I love meatloaf."

I handed her the flowers, and she said, "Thanks; they're beautiful. That was very thoughtful of you." She held the arrangement up to her face and breathed in the fragrance. Then she set the flowers on the granite countertop and said, "We're still about forty-five minutes away; why don't you boys grab a couple of beers and go out on the porch. I'll be along to join you in a few."

Bud dropped his empty bottle into a garbage bin that rolled out from under the counter, and then pulled open the door of the large built-in refrigerator. "Pick your poison, Jack. I've got Stella Artois or Budweiser, unless you'd like a cocktail."

"Stella would be great, please."

"Good man," he replied, popping the caps off a couple of bottles. "I wouldn't dare order this in town, for fear of the raft of shit I'd get about it, but I do really prefer it to most domestics."

He led me back out to the porch, and we took a couple of comfortable chairs. The front of the house faced south, and the sun had now moved far enough west that the porch and the area immediately in front of it were in the shade. The temperature had dropped a bit and with the slight breeze, it had turned into a very comfortable evening. "This is a pretty impressive place, you've got here, Bud. How many acres are you farming?"

"Thanks," he replied. "The entire operation is just a little over five thousand acres, which is thirteen or fourteen hundred larger than the average farm in South Dakota these days. Most of it's in corn and soybeans, although we do have a few cattle as well."

"No hogs?"

"Oh, Christ no." He laughed. "Too damned ugly and way too much work for what we'd get out of it."

"Well, I don't know a damned thing about farming, but to a city boy, it looks like you've done very well."

"Again, thanks, but of course I'm just continuing a tradition that started with my great-grandfather who homesteaded here with his family in 1877. When they first got here, they lived with four kids in a one-room house built of straw and clay with a sod roof. All of them worked like hell to build the foundation of this farm, and then my grandfather, who was the eldest son, ultimately took over.

"He was really the genius of the family. He managed to expand the farm a bit without incurring a lot of debt in the process, and then when the First World War broke out in Europe, it created a bonanza for American farmers. My grandfather worked himself and his kids as hard as he could to take advantage of it. He leased some land in addition to the home place here, and they literally planted fence post to fence post.

"Some farmers here and around the rest of the country too, of course, assumed that the good times would roll on forever and borrowed heavily to buy equipment and additional land. They also started buying luxuries that they hadn't been able to afford before. But then, of course, the war ended. European farmers went back into their own fields and the market for American crops in Europe nosedived, leaving a lot of those fellows in deep debt and even deeper trouble."

"Not your granddad, though?"

"No, sir. He was a very frugal guy and he understood that the high farm prices during the war weren't sustainable. By then, although they'd built a bigger and better house, they were still living and working very simply, and when the bottom fell out of the market, he was prepared for it because he'd saved his money during the war."

I took another hit on the Stella and said with a smile, "I hope to hell you're not going to tell me that he put it in the Security Bank."

He laughed. "No, thank God. He had a little money there and he was on the board of directors when the shit hit the fan. But he actually had invested most of his money in the stock market, which was pretty unusual for a farmer back then, and he left it there through most of the Twenties, riding the wave up along with all the big boys. Then he sold out in 1928, which was pretty close to the peak, and missed the crash."

"Sounds like he was a helluva lot smarter than some of those 'big boys' you mentioned."

"No, not really. It was more good luck than anything else. What happened was that by the late 1920s, a lot of farmers around here were in deep shit. They owed money to the banks and to the implement dealers and to the storekeepers in town and to anyone else who'd advance them credit. To be honest, of course, some of them *did* have what little savings they had in the Security Bank, and when that went under, so did some of them."

"For some reason, I feel like I should apologize for that."

"Well shit, Jack. I'm pretty damned sure that wasn't your fault any more than it was my Gramma's or anybody else's, save perhaps for your granddad and the auditors or whoever the hell should have caught up to him before the losses became so great that the bank couldn't be saved."

He sat for a moment, staring out across the fields in front of us and said, "Anyhow, the combination of all that meant that a man with some ready cash could pick up a lot of land around here, literally dirt cheap, and a lot of equipment as well. Grandad pulled his money out of the market, put it to work here, and managed to significantly increase the size of the farm."

"But what happened when the Depression hit?"

He shook his head. "Well, for farmers, of course, the Depression really began in about 1921 or '22. It just took a few years for the rest of the county to catch up. My grandfather let much of the land he'd bought lie fallow, and by then, the farm was basically self-sustaining. They grew their own food; they raised their own meat; and he sold just enough corn and beans to bring in a little cash to pay for the things they couldn't produce themselves. And since he didn't have any debts, he didn't have to worry about the bank or the taxman hounding him.

"Then, of course, once FDR got elected in '32, the government began paying farmers not to grow crops and there were other relief programs that helped. The REA, in particular, was a godsend."

"Sorry," I said. "Remember that I'm just a clueless city slicker. What the hell was the REA?"

He laughed again. "The Rural Electrification Administration. It was a program to bring electric power to rural areas. Up until then, people like my grandfather and his family were still cooking on wood stoves, heating themselves with fireplaces, reading by lantern light, and wandering out to the privy if they needed to go in the middle of the night—or at any other time, for that matter. The REA bringing electricity out here transformed their lives. They still had to go out to the privy, of course, but at least now, there could be an electric light in it."

I drained the last of the beer. "I admire the hell out of people like your grandfather, I would have never survived living like that."

Bud finished his beer and smacked me on the arm. "Of course you would have, you dumb shit. People did what they had to do in order to survive, and you would have too. Hell, a hundred years from now, people will no doubt look back and wonder how we ever survived without all the technology and other crap they'll have by then."

Just then, Becky pushed open the screen door and stepped out onto the porch with three fresh beers. Bud handed one to me, took one for himself and said, "Great timing, Beck; one of the many reasons why you're the best wife on the planet."

She snorted at that and sank into the chair next to Bud's. "You're so full of crap, I'll never understand why I put up with you. Besides which, maybe Jack here has a wife who's twice as great as I am."

I took a sip of the fresh Stella and said, "Not anymore, and from what little I've seen so far, I'm quite sure that neither of the ones I did have would've measured up to you, Becky."

"Christ, you're as full of it as Bud, here. Must be something that runs in your family."

"Bud was telling me about the history of your farm here. It's fascinating."

"You mean, he's boring you to tears, more likely,"

"No, honestly not. We'd gotten as far as the Thirties, and I'd love to hear what happened after that."

"Actually," Bud said, "there's really not much to tell after that. As I was saying, my grandfather managed to hold on through the Depression without nearly the problems a lot of his neighbors were having. Then World War II came along and solved the problem of farm prices again. While there were some periodic ups and downs, things were generally pretty good for us after that. My dad came along and took over the place when my granddad died. He added another five or six hundred acres, but like my grandad, he was very conservative about the way he did things, and so when it came time for me to take over, all I had to do was be a good steward to the operation they all had built."

He said the last a bit wistfully, picking at the label on his beer bottle, and I said, "You didn't have brothers or sisters competing for the job?"

He shook his head. In an even softer voice, he said, "Naw, that's really not the way it works in my family, or at least not the way it's worked up until now. I was the oldest son, and from the day I was born, it was just taken for granted that I'd grow up to work, first with my dad, and then to take the farm over from him. I have a younger sister and a brother after her, and neither one of them had any interest in it at all. They both wanted to get away from South Dakota as quickly as they could.

"My sister's married to a banker down in Denver and my little brother is a home builder out in Seattle. They each inherited twenty-four percent of the operation, leaving me with fifty-two. I'm free to run the place as I see fit and to pay profits out to my siblings when and if I feel the operation can afford it. But they're fine with that. They both got the lives that they wanted."

"Can I ask if you have kids who are going to take over?"

"Yes, you can ask and no we don't. That is, we *do* have kids, but they both have lives of their own and don't have any interest in farming. Our daughter, Kristi, is thirty, married with a couple of kids and lives in California where she went to college. Adam, our son, is twenty-seven and just graduated from law school and joined a firm in Chicago.

"When they were both still young, we sat each of them down and made it very clear that we expected them to follow their own path in life and that neither of them should feel any sort of obligation to continue this family tradition. I think they were both relieved, and frankly, so were Becky and me. We wouldn't have wanted to sentence either one of them to a life they didn't really want, just because it had been in the family for four generations before them."

He reached over and squeezed his wife's knee. "We're going to hang on and do this for maybe another five years or so and then sell out, which we'll be able to do without any problem. Then we're going to run away and be completely irresponsible and do exactly what we want with the rest of our lives."

"Sounds like a great plan to me," I said, finishing the second beer.

Becky finished her own beer, smiled, and patted her husband on the shoulder. "It *is* a great plan," she said, "but in the meantime, dinner's ready. Why don't we go in and eat?"

17.

The table in the dining area was set for three and Becky instructed Bud and me to sit down while she served the dinner. In addition to the meatloaf, there were mashed potatoes, gravy, and green beans, along with a nice bottle of pinot noir. I poured a little gravy over my meatloaf, took a first bite and said, "Wow, this is really amazing, Becky, and as I said, I'm a guy who's eaten a lot of meatloaf."

"I lucked out in that department too," Bud said. "Fifteen years ago, we built this house and that gargantuan, expensive kitchen over there. But the truth is, Becky's cooking was this good even when we were first married, living in a place with a little tiny kitchen, a crappy oven and a four-burner stove."

Becky took a sip of wine and set her glass on the table. "Well, to whatever extent that might be true, I owe it all to my mother. I learned by working with the best." Toying with the wine glass, she said, "So, Jack, Bud tells me that you're up here from Phoenix researching your family's history?"

I swallowed a bite of mashed potatoes and nodded. "I gather that you know at least something of all that."

"Only just a little that Bud's told me. His gramma was your grandad's younger sister, right?"

"Right."

"And he's the one who killed himself in the bank?"

"Yes. As I was telling Bud, I knew absolutely nothing about the man until just a few weeks ago. All the time I was growing up my mother and grandmother never talked about him. My mom died three months ago, and going through her things, I found a picture of him that she'd saved for years, hidden away in a box in a closet.

"I got curious and started digging around on the Internet. That's when I discovered that he'd embezzled money from the bank and then killed himself in the vault. I decided that I wanted to come up here and see the place for myself and maybe dig around and see how much of the story I could discover."

"So, what have you done so far?" she asked.

"I've been getting the lay of the land, and I've been to the Dugout, which was originally the bank where it happened. The guy who runs the place has a picture of my grandfather on the wall taken inside the bank."

Becky nodded and said, "Was that a little creepy?"

"Yeah, to be honest, it was. The vault where my grandfather died is now the bar's kitchen, and I have to tell you that, even though I never knew the guy, looking into that little room really affected me in a way that I wouldn't have expected. And I'm supposed to be a pretty hardened, cynical homicide detective."

"So, what else are you doing?" Bud asked.

"Well, I went to the sheriff's office hoping that there still might be a record of the investigation into his death, but, not surprisingly, their records don't go back that far. I was able to find the address of the house where my grandparents lived in Tyndall and I drove by there. I've spent a couple afternoons in the library, reading through newspapers from the period to get a sense of the town back then and to see what they might have had to say about all this business. I found a long story, which was actually very nice, about my grandfather's funeral. It made no mention at all of how he died or about any problems that might have existed at the bank.

"Then, of course, there were other articles about the money missing from the bank, about the failed effort to reorganize and reopen the bank, and ultimately about the depositors finally getting at least a little of their money back. I plan to spend another day or so there, continuing to work through the newspapers, but I also want to get over to the county museum and see if they might have anything that would be useful."

I polished off a second helping of meatloaf and potatoes and said, "Do you guys know anything about all of this? How did the story come down through your family, Bud, especially since your grandmother was my grandfather's sister?"

"To be honest, it really didn't. My gramma was something like ten years younger than your grandfather. By the time all that happened, she was married and living on a farm south of town. I have the impression that she was fairly close to her two sisters, but I don't know how close she might have been to your grandfather. My mom wasn't born until 1927, so of course, she had no independent memory of it at all.

"I first heard the story at a Thanksgiving dinner when I was about ten or so and some of the relatives were discussing it. The conversation was pretty brief, and from what I understood, apparently some of the people who got hurt when the bank failed took their anger out on the rest of your grandfather's family since he wasn't around to bear the brunt of it. But it also sounded to me like a lot of other people were sympathetic and understood that the blame rested with him and not with anybody else in the family, especially when it turned out that they obviously didn't have any of the missing money.

"As I said when we met in the café, a few people apparently shunned my gramma and, I'd assume, other members of the family for a while because of it. But by the time I came along, forty years after it all happened, it was pretty much ancient history, and nobody'd ever mentioned it in my presence until that Thanksgiving dinner. And I'm sorry to say that at that age, of course, the news that I was related to someone who had robbed a bank and then taken his own life like that was shocking, but it was also a little bit exciting, if you know what I mean."

"Yeah, I do. In fact, that was pretty much my reaction when I was a little kid and innocently asked my mom what had happened to my grandfather. She told me that he'd been killed in a bank robbery, and I naturally assumed that he'd been a customer in the bank or something like that and had been shot by the robbers. As a kid who played cops and robbers all the time, I thought it was pretty cool to think that my grandfather had been killed like that. But naturally, at five or six years old, I wasn't really capable of understanding the larger ramifications of it."

Becky got up and began clearing the table. I rose to help, but she waved me back into my chair and returned a couple of minutes later with a thick, delicious home-made chocolate pudding for dessert. I took a first bite and told her that it was fantastic. Again, she brushed away the compliment and I said to Bud, "Do you do any business with the Benson Farm Implement Company?"

"Yeah. We're basically a John Deere operation, and they're the nearest dealer. Their prices are fair, and they have a great service department, even if the guy who owns the place now is something of a dick."

Becky shot him a look, and he grinned. "Sorry, Beck. Of course, I should have said that he's something of a jerk. Why do you ask?"

"I'm curious about George Benson, the guy who founded the business. He was the head cashier at the Security Bank, and he was the one who discovered that my grandfather had been stealing from the bank. Instead of reporting the fraud as soon as he discovered it, he apparently gave my grandfather time to make things right, which, of course never happened.

"When the whole thing came out, the bank censored Benson for not reporting the thefts immediately, and then he lost his job when the bank failed. He worked at a farm implement dealership after that and then bought the business out and opened his own dealership in 1928. So, apparently he came out all right when all was said and done."

Bud shook his head. "Well, I don't know anything about that at all. I only know that the business has been in the family ever since it was founded. The guy who owns it now is somewhere in his late forties and inherited the business from his father about ten years ago.

"The father was a salt of the earth kind of guy and most everybody really liked him. The new guy is a cocky S.O.B., very full of himself, even though all he really did was have the business handed to him on a silver platter. He married some woman that he met in college, and who thinks that she's much too cultured and refined to be living in Tyndall, South Dakota. They spend a lot of time at their second home, which is someplace in California, and I have to say that nobody around here really misses them when they're gone."

"One other question," I said, folding my napkin and setting it on the table. "Do the names Hal Howard and Gary Checka mean anything to you guys?"

Becky and Bud looked at each other for a moment and then shook their heads at the same time. Bud said, "Off the top of my head, no. How do they figure into this?"

"Howard was the sheriff when my granddad died and the bank failed. Checka succeeded him at the end of that year. Apparently, they took whatever records they might have had with them when they left the office. It's a very small chance, but I was wondering if either one of them might still have relatives around here who would have held on to the records."

Again, my cousin shook his head. "I'll ask around, but again, the names don't ring a bell with me."

18.

By then it was closing in on ten o'clock. I assumed that as farmers, Bud and Becky probably had to be up around the crack of dawn, and I didn't want to overstay my welcome, so I declined the offer of an after-dinner drink and thanked them again for a great dinner and a very interesting conversation. They walked me to the door, and we stepped out onto the porch. By then it was dark, and lights had come on, automatically I assumed, illuminating the yard. Cody was waiting patiently by the door, basically in the same spot he'd taken three hours earlier. I leaned over, scratched his ears, and said, "It was very nice meeting you too, Cody."

Becky wrapped an arm around her husband's waist and said, "We enjoyed the evening, Jack. I really hope we'll see you again before you leave. I'd love to hear some of your stories about being a detective."

"Thanks. I'd enjoy seeing you guys again too, but I'm not sure those stories would be all that interesting."

We said our final goodnights and they waited while I got into the car and headed back down their road and out to the highway. The moon was a tiny crescent, barely clinging to the sky, and it was now completely dark in a way that the night was never fully dark in a metropolitan area like Phoenix. I had the road entirely to myself and turned on my bright lights which, out here, didn't really do that much to further illuminate the road. I drove along very slowly and carefully, thinking about the evening, and I was still about five or six minutes outside of Tyndall when I heard the crack of a shot and the rear window exploded behind me.

Instinctively, I slammed the gas pedal to the floor and a mile and a half down the road I slammed on the brakes and skidded around the corner from Willow back onto 20th, barely holding the Chrysler on the asphalt. Checking the rearview mirrors, I saw no lights coming behind me and so, assuming that I was safe at least for the time being, I slowed to forty-five and drove directly to the Sheriff's Department. There I found a male deputy, somewhere in his early thirties, sitting at the desk where the female officer had assisted me earlier in the day. I explained that someone had just taken a shot at me and he grabbed a pen and a notepad. "Where'd this happen?"

"Out on Willow Road, maybe three miles north of town, about five minutes ago."

"Did you get a look at the shooter?"

"No. I heard the shot and the window behind me shattered. I stomped on the gas, got the hell out of there, and came directly here."

Without having made any notes, the deputy picked the phone, punched a button, and said, "Sheriff, we have a problem out here."

He hung up the phone and a few seconds later a balding, middle-aged guy with thinning hair and a thick dark mustache walked down the hall. Dressed in dark blue jeans, boots and a uniform shirt with a badge hanging off his belt, the guy radiated a definite air of authority. He looked me up and down, then turned to the deputy and said, "What's the problem, Fred?"

"This gentleman says that someone just took a shot at him out on Willow north of town."

Turning back to me, the sheriff said, "And you are?"

"Jack Oliva, visiting from Arizona."

The guy stuck out his hand. "Stan Davis, Mr. Oliva."

I shook his hand and repeated the story I'd given the deputy. Davis listened carefully and then said, "Let's go take a look."

We walked down the hallway toward the door, and he said, "What brings you to Tyndall, Jack?"

"Just doing some genealogical work. My mother's family lived here in the 1920s, and I'm trying to fill in some of the blanks in my research."

"Oh, you're the guy who was in the office earlier today, wondering about our records. You told my deputy that you're related to Charles Kratina?"

"That's me. He was my grandfather."

We stepped through door and walked over to the Chrysler. Saying nothing, Davis took a long look at the shattered window and then slowly walked around the car. He stopped near the rear window on the passenger side and said, "Shot through and through."

I stepped up behind him, looked at the hole in the right rear window and said, "I was so panicked when it happened that I didn't even realize that the bullet had taken out this window too."

"You're a lucky man. If this guy's aim had been better, that bullet would have done quite a number on your head, assuming that is, that he was really trying to hit you and not just scare the living bejesus out of you." Looking from the window back to me, he said, "You pissed anybody off since you got into town, Jack?"

I shook my head. "I did keep the librarian maybe a couple of minutes after closing time this afternoon, but she really didn't strike me as the kind of woman who'd take a shot at me because of it."

"And you say this happened about three or four miles out of town? Do you mind me asking what you were doing out there?"

"No, not at all. I was having dinner with my cousin, Bud Daniels, and his wife. I got out there right at six and left a few minutes after ten. I was driving slowly south on Willow, heading back to my motel and minding my own business. There wasn't another vehicle anywhere around that I could see, and so I assume that the shooter must have been off in a field next to the highway."

"I have to say, Jack, that you seem to be pretty calm about this."

"Well, I guarantee that I wasn't all that calm in the moment, Sheriff, but although I hate to say it, this isn't the first time I've been shot at."

He gave me a look suggesting that he didn't like what he was hearing. "How's that, Mr. Oliva?"

"I'm a retired Phoenix homicide detective. I got shot at a couple of times while on the job and, I'm sorry to say, a few months ago some asshole actually hit me."

"You don't suppose the guy followed you up here and tried to finish the job?"

"Not a chance of that, Sheriff. He won't be shooting at anybody ever again."

Davis mulled that over for a minute, then said, "Do you have any I.D. you can show me?"

I dug out my wallet and handed him my Arizona driver's license along with a card officially identifying me as a retired member of the Phoenix P.D. He turned and held them up to the light so as to get a better look and then, apparently satisfied, handed the cards back to me.

"Well, Jack, since you're a detective, you obviously know that we're not going to learn anything by looking at your car. The bullet's long gone and I'm sure that the shooter is too, but why don't we drive out that way and you can show me where it happened."

I followed him across the parking lot to a Jeep that was outfitted with a light bar, a dashboard computer, a shotgun rack, and all the other paraphernalia that gets squeezed into a police vehicle these days. We pulled out of the lot and I directed him back in the direction of my cousin's farm. As we turned north onto Willow, I said, "Right up here, maybe two miles or so past the cemetery. There's a mailbox on the west side of the road that marks the spot pretty closely."

A couple of minutes later I pointed out the mailbox and Davis hit his flashing lights. We pulled off to the side of the road and got out of the Jeep. The sheriff produced a powerful flashlight which he played over the soybean field in front of us. Shaking his head, he said, "Well whoever your shooter is, he's obviously long gone, and if we go tramping out into that field in the dark, we'll probably destroy whatever evidence, if any, that he might have left out there. I'll send a couple of deputies out here in the morning to see if they can find anything in the light of day."

We returned to the Jeep and headed back toward town. Davis reached into his pocket, pulled out a package of Camels, and held it in my direction. "Do you smoke, Jack?"

"Not anymore, Sheriff, but go ahead. It certainly won't bother me."

He stuck a cigarette between his lips. "Nasty habit, I know, but I'm having a helluva time kicking it completely." He produced a Zippo lighter and fired up the cigarette. "Of course, legally, I'm not supposed to be smoking in an official vehicle, but I'm trusting that none of my deputies would be bold enough to ticket me for it."

I smiled at the thought. "I don't suppose that would be a good career move, would it?"

"Definitely not."

We drove along in silence for a couple of minutes, then he stubbed out what was left of the cigarette and said, "You're sure you have no idea who might have wanted to take a shot at you, Jack?"

"Well, Sheriff, if we were down in Phoenix, I could probably give you a long list of names. But I only got up here on Monday, and I don't know a soul. Or at least I didn't until I got here, and I'm quite sure I haven't angered anybody even in a small way, let alone so they'd want to do something like this. I did meet a guy at the Dugout last night who claimed that his grandfather was ruined by my grandfather and that he was still pissed about it. But he said what he had to say, and I didn't get the impression that he intended to do anything more about it. This afternoon, though, I did get an anonymous note at the library, apparently intended for me, warning me away from my project and telling me to get out of town."

"How's that?"

I told him how the note had been left at the library and how the librarian had assumed it was for me. I described the contents of the note and told him that I'd left it with the librarian for safekeeping. "Both the librarian and I got our fingerprints all over the envelope, but I was careful to take the note out of the envelope without getting any prints on it. If this business escalates, or if something untoward should happen to me, you might get the letter from her and see if you can raise any prints from it. But if nothing else happens, it probably wouldn't be worth your time to make the effort."

He thought about that for a minute or so, then said, "The guy from the Dugout, did you get his name?"

"Mack something. He said he was a heating and air conditioning repair man."

Davis nodded. "I know the guy. He's something of a blowhard, and I don't really think he'd have nerve enough to do something like this. Still, I guess you never know. I'll have a word with him tomorrow. As for the note you got, I think we'd better be safe rather than sorry, given that somebody just got off a shot in your direction. I'll stop by the library and pick up the note tomorrow. We'll send it off to the lab and see if they can get anything off of it.

"Of course, I suppose it's possible that this incident tonight had nothing to do with the threat you got. It could be that whoever it was, wasn't really shooting at you personally. Maybe it was just some asshole who'd had too much to drink and for the hell of it decided to fire off a shot in the direction of the first vehicle he saw coming down the highway."

"You get a lot of that around here?"

"More than I'd like, for damned sure, especially during hunting season. But usually the bastards are just shooting at road signs and at 'No Trespassing' signs. They're not normally firing at moving vehicles."

We pulled into the parking lot at the courthouse and walked back over to the Chrysler. Davis walked around the car again and said, "I imagine that the car rental people aren't going to be very happy with you."

"Probably not," I agreed. "Is there any place in town where I could get this fixed?"

He shook his head. "There are a couple of auto repair guys in town who could probably do the job for you, but of course they won't have the glass in stock. And by the time they get it from Sioux Falls or wherever, I imagine that it would be at least a couple of days."

"Well, I'm really not planning on being here that long, Sheriff. I guess I'll find some plastic to tape over the windows for the time being and then I'll either get it fixed on my way back through Sioux Falls or take my lumps with the rental agency."

Davis stuck out his hand. "Well, okay then. I guess that's about all we can do for tonight. I'd appreciate it if you'd stop by in the morning and make a formal report, just for the record, and I'll get somebody out there to poke around in that field. Who knows, maybe the dipshit who shot at you dropped his wallet in the process."

I shook his hand. "We should be so lucky. Thanks for your help, Sheriff, and I'll be sure to stop in tomorrow morning."

19.

There was no rain in the forecast and so I figured I could safely wait until morning to deal with the shattered windows in the Chrysler. I drove slowly down the street past the Welcome Inn, taking a careful look around. Seeing nothing that looked threatening or suspicious, I parked in front of my unit, grabbed my computer from the trunk and went inside.

I double-locked the door behind me, set the computer bag on the room's small desk, and poured myself a large shot of Elmer T. Lee from the flask I'd brought in my suitcase. Then I sat down on the bed, leaned back against the headboard, and tried to figure out who in the hell might have taken a shot at me and why.

I really couldn't believe that Mack, whatever-his-last-name-was, had done it. After being a cop as long as I was, you get a sense about people, and the sheriff's assessment of the guy dovetailed with my own. But then, as the sheriff said, you never really know.

I had more than a little trouble believing that some liquored-up jerk had simply taken a random shot at a passing car, but as I'd told the sheriff, it was also hard to imagine that I'd antagonized anybody that badly, other than maybe Mack, at least anybody here in South Dakota. And who in the hell had left the note warning me to get out of town?

By now, any number of people knew that I was up here looking into my family's history, and many of them also knew that I was related to Charles Kratina. I'd told a few people that myself, and I assumed that the bartender at the Dugout had told the story of the "Ghost's Grandson" to everybody who'd walked into the place in the last couple of days. But why the hell should anyone care about that, especially at this late date?

And who knew that I'd be spending the evening out at my cousin's farm? Bud, for sure, but he'd issued the invitation in front of Meg, the waitress, and several customers in the café, any one of whom might have overheard the conversation. It was also possible that someone had been watching my movements and had simply followed me out of town and then set up to take a shot at me, assuming that I'd eventually be coming back the same way. But again, why? And were they really trying to kill me or were they simply attempting to scare me into leaving town?

After turning the matter over for twenty or thirty minutes, neither Elmer nor I had come up with any good answers and so I decided to hit the sack. I also decided that, starting tomorrow morning, I was going to be paying a lot more attention to whatever might be going on around me.

20.

I awoke a little after seven, hauled myself out of bed, and then shaved, showered, and dressed, ready to get the day under way. I hung my computer bag off my shoulder and headed for the door. Then I stopped, thought things over for a couple of seconds and set the computer bag back on the desk. I fired up the computer, dug a flash drive out of one of the pockets in the bag, and backed up the notes I'd made since arriving in town. I stuck the backup drive in my pants pocket then walked out and locked the door behind me.

The poor Chrysler looked even worse in the cold light of day. The left rear window was almost completely blown out, and there was a huge hole in the right rear window, with the remaining glass spider-webbed around the hole. Fragments of glass were scattered all over the back seat and on the floor between the seats.

I'd gassed up yesterday at a convenience store a couple of blocks away and remembered that they had a coin-operated vacuum cleaner hanging off the wall of the store. I drove up the street and parked in front of the vacuum. The clerk on duty was a heavy-set young woman, maybe twenty-one or twenty-two, with a nose ring and an amazing number of tattoos. I bought a package of plastic sheeting and a roll of duct tape and explained that someone had broken a window out of my car.

She changed a five-dollar bill into quarters and loaned me a broom and a large dustpan. Back outside, I opened the rear doors of the car and used the broom handle to punch the remaining glass out of the windows and into the dustpan. I then swept the glass off the back seat into the pan and dumped it all into a large trash barrel. I pumped four quarters into the vacuum which, thankfully, was fairly powerful, and went carefully over the seat and the rear floor.

After another four quarters worth, I was pretty sure that I'd gotten all the glass out of the car. I returned the broom and dustpan to the young woman, thanking her for her assistance. Then I covered each of the windows with the plastic sheeting, stretching the plastic tight and taping it down firmly along all the edges. I knew that the plastic would vibrate and that it was going to be noisy as hell, especially at highway speeds, but there wasn't much else I could do at this point.

* * *

Meg was behind the counter when I got to the café for my morning coffee, dressed today in a red tee shirt and a pair of jeans that fit her as snugly as the shorts she'd been wearing yesterday. The distinct aroma of cooked bacon and freshly baked rolls hung in the air. A number of patrons followed my progress from the door to the counter, without disguising their interest, and Meg set a steaming mug of coffee in front of me before I could even sit down. "Sounds like you had quite the adventure last night."

I took a sip of the coffee, which tasted especially good this morning, and said, "News seems to travel fast around here."

"Not all that fast, actually, but one of the sheriff's deputies was in for breakfast this morning and mentioned the fact that someone had taken a shot at you last night."

"Probably not at me so much. The sheriff seems to think that somebody who might have had a little too much to drink just decided to take a shot at a passing car."

"Well, I'm sure that the Chamber of Commerce isn't going to like that, what with you being a visitor up here and all."

"No. All in all, it doesn't seem like the kind of thing that would encourage tourism."

She patted my arm. "Whatever. I'm sure glad they missed, Honey; it's nice to see you back here healthy and all in one piece."

She moved down the counter to tend to another customer, and the rest of the patrons returned to their breakfasts and conversations. By the time I finished my coffee, the place had cleared out a bit and no one was sitting within four stools of me along the counter. Meg walked down and poured me another half a cup. As quietly as I could, I said, "I don't suppose there are any gun dealers in town, are there, Meg?"

She leaned across the counter, closing the distance between us. In a low voice she said, "You mean, just in case someone *wasn't* shooting at you accidentally?"

"Right. I have a couple of guns at home, but of course I couldn't bring them with me on the plane. All of a sudden, I'm feeling sort of naked without one."

She nodded. "Well, there aren't any shops in town that sell guns, but there are a couple of guys I know here who buy and sell guns on a regular basis."

"Could you point me in their direction?"

She stood up straight again and said, "Hang on a sec, Hon."

She grabbed her purse from under the counter and retrieved her cellphone. She disappeared back in the direction of the kitchen for three or four minutes, then returned and slid a piece of paper with a name, address, and a phone number on it across the counter. "You might want to try Bruce here. He's a nice guy and he has a reputation for being fair. I called him and told him you might be coming along. He's at home now and says he'll be there for another hour or so."

21.

Meg gave me directions to the guy's house, which she said was only about three minutes away. I thanked her and paid the check, leaving a very generous tip. Then I got back in the Chrysler and made a quick trip to the Security State Bank where I used the cash machine at the front of the building. Back in the car, I found the guy's house without any trouble. It was on a quiet, residential street, although to be honest, I'd yet to see a street in Tyndall that wasn't quiet. The house was about due for a coat of paint, but the lawn was well-tended, and everything about the house appeared neat and tidy.

I hadn't even had a chance to ring the bell before the door was opened by a huge man who looked like he'd just walked out of the woods somewhere. He had to go an easy six-four and two hundred and fifty pounds. Dressed in boots, jeans, and a plaid flannel shirt, he was sporting long dark hair and a full, bushy beard that was flecked with grey. Looking at me through the screen door, he said, "You Jack?"

"Right."

He unlatched and opened the screen door, then stuck out his hand. "Bruce Gentry."

I shook his hand and introduced myself, then followed him into a sparsely furnished living room. He closed the door, locking it behind him. Then he turned to me and said, "Meg said you might be interested in buying a gun?"

"Right. As I told her, I've got a couple back home in Phoenix, but I couldn't bring them on the plane with me when I came up here. I'm feeling kind of vulnerable without one, if you know what I mean."

"I do, absolutely. So, what were you looking for, Jack?"

"A pistol, preferably a semi-automatic."

He nodded. "Something you can carry concealed?"

"Right."

"I've got a couple of Glocks that might fit the bill. Hang on a sec."

He disappeared down the hall and returned a couple of minutes later, carrying two pistols. Handing me one, he said, "Your basic G27, Gen 3, .40 caliber. Small, lightweight, but still very powerful. 9-round capacity."

Still holding the other gun, he showed it to me. "The G43, Gen 4, the smallest 9mm that Glock makes. A tad lighter than the 27, but only six in the mag."

He watched as I popped the magazine and tested the mechanisms of the G27 and then repeated the process with the G43. Both worked smoothly and, though used, had obviously been well-cared for. Still holding the G27, I said, "What are you asking for this one?"

He pretended to think about it for a couple of seconds, then said, "I could let you have that one for four hundred. Since this is a friendly, person-to-person sale, we wouldn't have to do any paperwork."

My turn to pretend to think. I waited about five or ten seconds and then said, "How about three-fifty, cash, for the gun and, say, twenty rounds to go with it?"

Without hesitating, he said, "Three seventy-five, including the ammo. That's the best I can do, Jack."

I agreed to his price and counted out the money. Gentry left the room for another minute, then came back and handed me the gun and a box of Remington HTP Hollow Points. I handed him the cash, took the gun and the ammo, and said, "Thanks, Bruce. I appreciate it."

"My Pleasure, Jack."

I stood there, contemplating my purchases for a moment, then said, "You wouldn't happen to have an ankle holster that would work with this gun, do you, Bruce?"

"I've got one that's good for either the 26 or the 27. Let me show you."

He disappeared for another couple of minutes then returned with a small, black holster with a wide elastic band that was secured by Velcro. Handing it to me, he said, "This is great for concealing the weapon since the gun rests on the inside of your ankle, rather than on the outside. Assuming that you're right-handed, you'd probably want to wear it on your left ankle to get at it the quickest. As you can see, this is a new one, and I can let you have it for another forty."

"That seems fair," I agreed, and handed him another two twenties.

Gentry walked me to the door, then paused and said, "I gather you only plan on using that weapon while you're up here visiting, probably for target practice or something?"

"Something like that."

"But if you couldn't bring your own guns up here on the plane, you probably can't take that one back home with you."

"No, I guess not."

"Well, then, if you wanted to stop by on your way out of town, maybe I could take it off your hands, assuming it hasn't been badly used."

"Maybe, Bruce; we'll see."

We shook hands and he watched me down the steps and out to my car. Figuring that it would be a bad idea to carry a concealed weapon into the Sheriff's office, I locked my new gun in the trunk for the time being and headed off in the direction of the courthouse.

* * *

The young female deputy was on the front desk again and I told her that I needed to file a report about an incident last night. She nodded. "The sheriff told me I should expect you."

She called up a form on her computer and said, "It's probably easier for both of us if I just do this on the computer rather than printing out the form and having you fill it in by hand."

She entered my personal information into the form and then took down the basics of the incident. It only took a few minutes, after which she printed out a copy and gave it to me to review and sign. It all looked good, so I signed the document and handed it back. She set it in a basket on her desk and as she did, the sheriff walked through the door and said, "Good timing, Mr. Oliva. Why don't you come into my office for a minute?"

I followed him down the hall to a small but exceptionally neat office that was furnished with an ancient oak desk and chair, a bank of file cabinets, a bookshelf and a couple of guest chairs. A large window to the left of the desk looked out onto the courthouse lawn, which appeared to be overdue for a mowing. Davis took the chair behind the desk and motioned me in the direction of one of the guest chairs. "I had a couple of deputies get out into that field this morning," he said, "and I'm afraid that they didn't come up with anything that's going to give us a clue as to who might have taken a shot at you last night, Jack."

"I'm sorry to hear that, Sheriff, but I can't say I'm all that surprised."

"Didn't figure you would be. It's clear that someone walked out into that field within the last couple of days from the gravel road alongside it and settled into a spot that would give him a clear view of the road. But unfortunately, he didn't leave anything behind that's going to help us, not even a decent footprint. I also talked to Mack Thompson who appears to have a solid alibi for ten o'clock last night and who insists that, while he might be sore about what your grandfather did back then, he sure as hell wouldn't take a shot at you for it."

He paused for a moment, then looked me squarely in the eye. "You're sure you can't think of anyone else who might have wanted to take a shot at you?"

I returned the look. "None, Sheriff. And if I did, you'd be the first person I'd tell."

I waited a second while he absorbed that and then said, "Let me ask you a question, Sheriff. As you and a lot of other people in town now seem to know, I'm up here looking into my family's history, including my grandfather who committed suicide in Tyndall over ninety years ago. Is there any reason why that should make somebody nervous?"

"Not that I can think of, but then my family's only been here since the 1950s, and I know nothing at all about your family or your grandfather's suicide, except what you told my deputy yesterday morning. I gather that your grandfather had something to do with a bank failing here in town back in the Twenties?"

"Right. He embezzled the money that caused the bank to fail and then shot himself when it all started unravelling."

Davis shrugged. "I'd assume that a lot of people would have been pretty angry about it when it happened, but it's hard to imagine that there'd be anyone around carrying a grudge after all this time, let alone who'd think it would be a good idea to take your grandfather's crimes out on you."

"That's certainly what I'd think, Sheriff. Hell, maybe your guess about someone just taking a random shot at a passing car is really what happened, and it has nothing to do with me personally."

"Let's hope so, Jack. But keep me posted if anything else should happen."

I rose and offered him my hand. "I will, Sheriff, and thanks. But you will be sure to let me know if somebody gets a sudden attack of conscience and comes in and confesses?"

That brought a laugh. "I will. But I wouldn't bet my lunch money on the chances."

22.

It was only a little after eleven o'clock when I left the Sheriff's office, which meant that it was still two hours before I could get back into the library. I decided that I would use some of the time to have an early lunch and then finally pay a visit to my grandfather's grave. I found a parking place in front of the café and was halfway to the front door when I thought about the gun that was still locked in the trunk.

I couldn't imagine that I'd be needing it either in the café or in the library, but then, why in the hell had I bothered to buy it if I wasn't going to be prepared to use it? I'd feel like the Chump of the Century if somebody stuck a gun in my ribs and marched me out of the café, or if, God forbid, the librarian pulled a shotgun on me while I was reading the newspapers, and all the while my new Glock was locked out of the way in the trunk.

Deciding to be better safe than sorry, I walked back to the car, took a quick look around to make sure that no one was watching, and opened the trunk. The shopping bag from the convenience store was still lying there, and so I dumped the remaining plastic sheeting and the duct tape out into the trunk and slipped the gun, the holster, and nine bullets into the sack. I locked the trunk again and carried the sack into the cafe.

Standing behind the counter, Meg gave me a smile and said, "Coke?"

"Perfect," I replied, pointing down the hall toward the restroom door. "I'll just be a minute"

"Right."

I walked past the counter and into the restroom. I locked myself in, then took the gun out of the bag and loaded the nine

126

bullets into the magazine without chambering a round. I slipped the gun into the holster and then strapped it to my left ankle and pulled the leg of my jeans down over it. With the gun resting on the inside of my ankle, it was virtually invisible under the jeans and, satisfied, I dumped the shopping bag into the trash and walked back out to the counter.

Meg had set my Coke in front of an empty stool and I ordered a tuna salad sandwich to go with it. Ten minutes later, she served the sandwich and said, "Did you manage to hook up with Bruce?"

"Yes, thanks. Again, I appreciate the referral."

"Glad to help," she said, as she moved on down to take another order.

The place was filling up as noon approached, and so I finished my lunch fairly quickly. Deciding to delay having a piece of pie until dinner, I paid up and said goodbye to Meg. Back in the car, I fired up the engine and backed out of my parking space. Watching the rearview mirror for any approaching traffic, I noticed a light gray car which appeared to be idling a half a block south down the street. The car had a front license plate in an odd yellow color, and I remembered seeing the same car behind me earlier in the morning while I was on my way from the sheriff's office to the cafe.

It seemed highly unlikely that the same car would have been behind me by accident twice within an hour, but I couldn't imagine why in the world anyone would be tailing me through the streets of Tyndall, South Dakota. Just to make sure that I wasn't imagining things, I turned left onto Eighteenth and drove west a block to Laurel. I turned right onto Laurel and drove north to Twentieth. There I turned right, now heading east to Willow, which would take me to the cemetery. The car stayed with me all the way through the maneuver and all the way out to the cemetery. Either the guy was a total novice at following someone, or he didn't particularly care that he might be spotted in the process.

As I reached the gate to the cemetery, I parked by the side of the road and my shadow pulled off about thirty yards behind me. Mindful of the fact that somebody had taken a shot at me less than twenty-four hours earlier, I leaned over and pulled the Glock from my ankle holster. I jacked a round into the chamber and stuck the gun into the waistband of my jeans. Then I pulled my shirt out to cover the gun and walked back to the gray car, which turned out to be a Honda of indeterminate vintage.

The guy behind the wheel was barely more than a kid, maybe twenty-five or so, with blond hair shaved close on the sides and left longer on top. He was wearing sunglasses and as I approached the car, he appeared to be studiously reading a newspaper. I tapped on the window and he looked up at me. I couldn't tell if the surprise that registered on his face was genuine or feigned, but that hardly mattered.

I made the universal sign for "Roll down your window, asshole," and he did. He set the paper aside on the passenger seat and said, "Can I help you?"

"Indeed, you can, Son. And you can start by telling me why in the hell you've been following me around town this morning."

His voice seemed to go up a notch. "Following you? I'm not following you."

"Yeah, you are and you're doing a piss-poor job of it. I want to know why."

"I'm not following you, and why the hell would I? You should just mind your own damned business."

"Believe me, kid, I'm more than happy to do just that, at least until someone like you sticks his nose into it. So, tell me, if you're not following me, how did you manage to get here at the same moment I did? And what are you doing here? Did you maybe come out to visit your grandma's grave? If that's the case, we can go into the cemetery together."

The kid fired up the engine and turned to me. "Fuck you, old man. I'm not going anywhere with you."

With that, he dropped the car into gear and sped off down the road, spewing gravel behind him. I went back to my own car and jotted down his license number. Then I transferred the Glock back to its holster, pulled out my cell phone and called the sheriff's office. The dispatcher transferred me to Stan Davis, and I wished him a good afternoon. "I'm not sure what this might mean, Sheriff, and I have no idea if it's related to the incident last night, but I seem to have picked up a tail this morning."

"The hell you say."

"Yeah. Some guy, middle twenties, blonde hair, maybe five-seven and one-fifty. Driving a light gray Honda Accord." I gave him the plate number and said, "The guy followed me from your office to the café this morning, then from there out to the Czech National Cemetery.

"I braced him, and of course he insisted that he wasn't following me. Then he told me to fuck off and raced away. I'm not really asking you to do anything about it, but I did want to bring you up to date just in case somebody with better aim than the guy from last night takes another shot at me while I'm up here in your jurisdiction."

"Appreciate that, Jack. It will make my life a helluva lot easier and give me a place to start in case we find you by the side of the road with a bullet or two in you. In the meantime, I'll run the plate just to see who we're dealing with here, and if it's anybody I think you should be worried about I'll get back to you."

* * *

I thanked the sheriff, then got out of the car and walked through the open gate into the cemetery. A man who looked to be the caretaker was clipping some grass around the fence and I asked him if he might know where my grandfather's grave was. He thought for a moment, looking out over the rows of graves, and then said, "Sure." Nodding his head, he said, "It's right over here."

He led me down several rows of gravestones and walked to his right another twenty feet or so. Then, pointing his hand at the ground, he said, "Right there," and I got another huge surprise.

My grandfather's gravestone was a small, flat marker with his name, and the dates of his birth and death, just as I had seen on the website for South Dakota Gravestones. But right next to his stone was my grandmother's, an identical marker with her birth and death dates. I knew that my grandmother had been buried in Tyndall, and I remembered that my mother had ridden the train carrying Grandma's casket back to South Dakota. But I always assumed that she had been buried in the Catholic cemetery and had no idea that she had been laid to rest alongside my grandfather.

I assumed that my grandmother must have reserved the space next to my grandfather at the time of his death, nearly forty years before her own. For the last few weeks, I'd also assumed that she'd remained angry at him for the rest of her life for the actions he had taken that had destroyed their family. If not, why had she spent all those years appearing to ignore his memory? But the fact that she had elected to be buried beside him suggested that she had not remained angry with him and, perhaps, at some point had forgiven him. Somehow, it made me happy to see that they'd been reunited in death, but I sure as hell couldn't begin to explain how odd the whole situation continued to seem.

I stood there for twenty minutes or so, thinking about my grandmother and regretting the fact that I'd never had the chance to know my grandfather. Then, although I'd long since lost any belief in God or in the Hereafter, I said a silent prayer for the two of them and headed on back to the library.

23.

I got to the library right on time, parked in my usual spot in front of the building and locked up the Chrysler. I couldn't imagine why in the hell I bothered, given that anyone could simply pull the plastic off one of the back windows and have access to anything he might want in the car. I had my computer bag in hand and thus there wasn't anything of value left in the car, but still, it was a matter of habit.

Tracy, the librarian, wished me a good afternoon, and said that the sheriff had just been in to pick up the note that had been left for me. "He said that you had some trouble last night."

"Yes, although I don't know how serious it was, and I have no idea whether or not it was connected to the note you found yesterday. But the sheriff decided to have the note checked out of an abundance of caution."

"Do you think there's any chance he might be able to figure out who sent it?"

"I'd say the chances are small. If the person who wrote the note was careless and left fingerprints on the page, and if his or her fingerprints are on file for some reason, then I guess it would be possible. But I'm betting that whoever did it was careful enough not to touch the paper with his or her bare hands, and so the crime lab probably won't be able to provide the sheriff with any leads."

"Well, let's hope they weren't that careful. It would be nice to think that they wouldn't get away with threatening you like that."

"Let's hope," I said, "but I'd better get back to work."

I left the librarian at her desk still puzzling over the situation and returned to my research. I was continuing to work my way through the local newspapers, and I'd now made my way to the issues for 1927, without learning anything more about my grandfather, the bank failure or the death of the former sheriff. The farm economy continued to be in the dumpster and the newspaper's editor continued his effort to put the best face on the situation, assuring readers that things would be looking up shortly.

The paper changed ownership on September 1, 1927, and the new owners rechristened the paper as *The Bon Homme County Register.* On September 27, they ran an article indicating that the State Banking Department had paid another ten percent dividend to the creditors of the Security Bank. "This dividend makes a payment of 30 percent that has been returned to the depositors after the bank closed."

The paper noted that "This payment distributes about $60,000 in this community, which ought to help financial conditions and increase the amount of exchange in business channels." Ever optimistic, the paper expressed the hope that "with the good corn crop in sight and the generally fair prices prevailing for practically all farm products, it looks as though the debtors of the bank would be able to make substantial payment on their notes, holding out a hope that in the not too far distant future, the Receiver can report another dividend payment."

I'd been at it for about thirty minutes when a guy stepped up to the table where I was working, pulled out a chair and sat down like he owned the place. Fifty years old, maybe, wearing clothes and a haircut that he clearly gotten somewhere other than in Tyndall, South Dakota. Otherwise fit and trim, his ruddy face suggested that he might be a heavy drinker, and the slight tremor in his hand made the cop in me wonder if he might also be abusing drugs.

He crossed his right leg over his left knee and leaned back in the chair. "You must be Mr. Oliva."

I pushed my computer away a bit and leaned back in my own chair. "And you must be Alex Benson."

He sat for a moment, continuing to appraise me, then said, "My, we *have* been busy, haven't we?"

I didn't really think that he expected an answer to that, and so I said, "What brings you to the library, Mr. Benson?"

"Curiosity, Mr. Oliva. I understand that you've been prying around, digging into my family's background, and I wanted to know why."

"Well, I'm sorry to say that you've been misinformed. I'm researching my own family's history and I've explored your family's history only as it relates to mine."

He uncrossed his legs, shifted in his chair, and closed the gap between us a bit. "Well, I'm sorry to say, but that's not the way I hear it. I understand that you've been poking around, asking questions about my great-grandfather. Why would you possibly be interested in him?"

"Your great-grandfather and my grandfather worked together at the Security Bank, back in the 1920s. Your great-grandfather was the one who discovered that my grandfather had embezzled money from the bank, so I'm naturally curious about him."

"Well, you have no damned reason to be. Your fuckin' grandfather ruined the bank and cost my great-grandfather his job. My great-grandfather was lucky to land on his feet."

"Damned lucky, as I hear it."

"And what's that supposed to mean?"

"Just that. He managed to catch on at the farm implement dealership and then just as the place was going under, he was fortunate to inherit enough money for him to buy the dealership and set him and his family up for life."

Benson tensed up and leaned forward again. In a low voice he said, "And just what are you implying?"

"Absolutely nothing at all. As I said, your great-grandfather turned out to be a very fortunate man."

133

He sat back and considered me for a moment, then he leaned forward again. "I understand you've been telling people that you think my great-grandfather was involved with your grandfather in stealing money from the bank."

Shaking my head, I said, "That's absolutely not true. Who in the world told you that?"

"None of your business, and it damned well better not be true."

"Listen, Mr. Benson, I've seen absolutely nothing in my research to suggest that your great-grandfather might have been involved in the thefts. I certainly have not accused him of anything like that, and I can't imagine why anyone would have said otherwise. I'd suggest that you go back to whoever it was and find out."

He waited a moment, apparently appraising my response, then said, "How long do you plan to be in town, Mr. Oliva?"

"Until I'm finished with my research, Mr. Benson."

"Well, I'd urge you to wrap up your 'research' fairly soon, and I'd strongly encourage you to confine your attention to your own family. If you continue to poke around in my family's business, I'll see that you have cause to regret it. I have a great deal of influence in this town and I won't hesitate to use it if I have to."

With that, he got up, pushed his chair back, and walked quickly out of the building. The librarian had been sitting at her desk across the room and had obviously witnessed the conversation, even if she couldn't hear all of it. She watched Benson leave, then looked at me and raised her eyebrows. I stood and walked over to her desk. "Does Mr. Benson patronize the library on a regular basis?"

She shook her head. "I don't think he's ever been in here before. He's never struck me as being much of a reader."

"But he *is* a big man around these parts?"

Smiling, she said, "He certainly likes to think so, but he'll never be the man his father was, not in this town or any other."

"I gather that the company he inherited is very important to the community, though."

"Oh, definitely. They're the biggest employer in town and a significant factor in the local economy, such as it is these days. The earlier generations of Bensons were also very generous in terms of supporting this library and the community generally. Unfortunately, the current Mr. Benson doesn't have the same level of commitment to the community, and the town is suffering a bit as a result."

"I gather that you've known him for a while?"

"Practically all my life, although he's never taken any notice of me. As you will have observed, this is a very small town and as a practical matter, everyone knows everyone else. Alex was four years ahead of me in school, and since he came from perhaps the most prominent family in town, he was something of a Big Man on Campus at our high school, even though it was a very small campus."

As attractive as the woman was in her middle forties, I found it hard to imagine that Alex Benson and most other men would not have taken notice of her, either in high school or in the present day, but I let that pass and said, "Was he a good student?"

"Average at best. Alex was good enough to play football for a very small high school, but not nearly good enough to play at the college level. And in high school, he was much more accomplished on the party circuit than he was in the classroom. He wound up going off to one of the lesser state universities in the California system and ultimately did manage to graduate. The rumor around town, though, suggested that it was a close call and that Alex applied himself hard enough to graduate only because his father threatened not to bring him into the business if he failed to earn a degree."

"I understand that he still spends quite a bit of time in California."

"As much as he possibly can, I gather. He married a woman from Long Beach who much prefers southern California to southern South Dakota, and Alex appears to be of the same mind. They have a totally inappropriate house that they built at the far north end of Maple Street, but Mrs. Benson spends as little time there as possible, and Mr. Benson spends not much more than that. He seems to be here only as often as the business actually requires his presence."

There seemed nothing more to say and so I went back to the microfilm reader, wondering who might have told Alex Benson that I thought his great-grandfather could have been complicit in my grandfather's thefts, assuming that someone actually had told him that.

For the last couple of days, there had been a tiny voice, lurking in my subconscious, suggesting that George Benson, Senior, *had* been very lucky and that his mysterious uncle had died at a very fortuitous moment, not all that long after the money stolen from the Security Bank had totally disappeared. But I hadn't even allowed it to become a conscious thought, let alone suggest to anyone else that Benson's inheritance might not have come from an uncle, but rather from the bank.

Thinking about it, I decided to scroll forward to the newspapers for May 1928. A front-page article in the May 22 edition reported that George Benson had assumed ownership of Tyndall Farm Implements and had renamed the business the Benson Farm Implement Company. The paper noted that the original owner, a man named Alfred Thompson, had decided to leave the business to "pursue other opportunities," and that he had sold the business to Benson, who had been the General Manager of the firm "for the last several years."

Benson was quoted as saying that he was "very pleased to have this opportunity to serve the farmers of Bon Homme County and beyond." He indicated that he planned to significantly expand the business and to acquire new lines of farm equipment in order to provide the firm's customers with a variety of products from which to choose. He announced that the service department would also be expanded and that local farmers "need look no further than the Benson Company" for all their equipment needs.

The editor thanked the previous owner for his service to the community and wished him the best of luck in his future endeavors. He expressed confidence in Benson as a man who "knows the business inside and out," and who could be counted upon to do great things with it. The paper made no mention of how Benson had acquired the capital necessary to buy the business.

I scrolled forward, looking for other articles about the company. I found Benson's name in several articles, touting his contributions to the community and as the months passed, the Benson Farm Implement Company became one of the paper's most prominent advertisers. An article in the edition on April 4, 1930, noted that the firm had acquired the John Deere line of tractors and other equipment, which Benson described as "the industry leader in quality agricultural equipment."

I was rapidly running out of time and so began skimming quickly though subsequent editions of the paper, looking for any additional news about the affairs of the Security Bank. In mid-January, 1930, the paper reported that a fifth dividend of ten percent had been paid to the bank's creditors, meaning that just short of five years after the bank failed, those depositors who had been able to hang on to their certificates now had fifty percent of their money back. But with the Depression now in full bloom, I wondered if they would ever see another payment, let alone be made whole.

By late 1931, whatever optimistic tone the paper had once maintained had been swamped by the continuing bad economic news. The paper now regularly contained articles about falling farm prices and farm relief programs. The number of foreclosures in the county was increasing rapidly and merchants were reducing prices in the hope of attracting customers. On October 22, the paper reported that the bank at Tabor had failed, leaving only four banks operating in the county out of an original total of eleven. One of the four was Tyndall's only other bank, The First National Bank, but then it too failed in July 1932, due to "depleted reserves and frozen assets," bringing additional grief and misery to the community.

If that weren't bad enough, the effort to collect the monies owed to the Security Bank had apparently slowed to a trickle, making it impossible to pay another ten percent dividend to the creditors. At the end of October 1932, the paper noted that the bank's depositors and other creditors would receive a dividend of three-quarters of one percent. In a letter to the creditors, the Superintendent of Banks, E. A. Ruden, noted that "Eventually there may be a final small dividend paid," after certain other assets were liquidated. It thus appeared that, after all was said and done, over a period of seven years, the depositors ultimately got back just a touch over fifty percent of the money they had entrusted to the Security Bank of Tyndall.

In better news, however, on November 1, 1932, a new bank, The Security State Bank of Tyndall, opened for business, renting space in the former Security Bank Building. The paper reported that the formation of the new bank, "is expected to help business conditions here considerably."

Happily for the people of Tyndall and the surrounding area, they now finally had a bank that would survive down to the present day, and in fairly short order the creation of the Federal Deposit Insurance Corporation under President Roosevelt's New

Deal, would insure the money they deposited in the bank. They and most other Americans would never have to worry about losing their money in a failed bank again.

I assumed that future editions of the paper would continue to make occasional mention of both George Benson and his company and about the local banking situation, but I decided that I'd now done about all I could with the newspapers. A few minutes before five, I backed up my files to the flash drive and slipped the drive back into my pocket. I rolled the microfilm back onto its reel, slipped it into the box and returned it to the librarian. I thanked her for her help over the last few days and she said, "I hope you found what you were looking for."

"I did learn quite a few things that I hadn't found on the Internet, I'm not sure it was everything I might have been looking for, though. I have been hoping to get into the heritage museum, but I've been by there several times and they don't seem to have regular hours."

"No, they don't. The staff is entirely volunteer, and unfortunately there are only a few people now who take an interest in it. They work there when they can spare the time, but they don't have regularly scheduled hours. If you like, I'd be happy to call one of them, though, and explain that you'd like to see what they might have there."

I expressed my thanks and the woman checked a number in her small address book, then punched a number into the phone on her desk. Someone, apparently named Anna, answered the call, and the librarian explained that I was in town for only a few days doing research on my family and that I was hoping to see what the museum might have in its collection. She listened to the person's response and then looked up to me. "Would you be free to go down there around nine-thirty tomorrow morning?"

"That would be perfect."

She relayed the information and then concluded the call. Grabbing a piece of scratch paper, she wrote the name, "Anna Nelson" followed by the woman's phone number. Handing it to me, she said, "Anna says she'd be happy to meet you there tomorrow morning. She's been meaning to get over there and do some work herself, and she can tell you whether or not they might have anything that would be useful to you."

* * *

I stuck the note in my pocket, thanked the librarian again for her help, and decided on a lark to get a look at Alex Benson's house, wondering why the librarian had described it as "totally inappropriate."

I locked my computer bag in the trunk and drove over to Maple Street. There I turned north and followed the road to the far end of town. I had no trouble finding the house that must have belonged to the Bensons, which sat on a very large lot on the west side of the street. I also had no trouble imagining why the librarian had described the house as she did.

In a town that consisted mostly of relatively small clapboard houses roofed with asphalt shingles, the Bensons had built a huge, rambling stucco home with a red tile roof and a three-car garage. It would have fit perfectly into a neighborhood in southern California, but in Tyndall, South Dakota it stuck out like Gulliver among the Lilliputians.

The house was surrounded by a low stucco fence that matched the exterior of the house. Wrought-iron gates blocked access to the asphalt driveway, and a small Mercedes convertible sat parked in front of the garage. A landscaper's truck with a Yankton address on the door was parked just off the street in front of the house, and a guy on a riding mower was slowly cutting the huge lawn that separated the house from the street.

I sat there, idling the car in front of the house for a couple of minutes, wondering what the other residents of Tyndall must have thought of the house and of the couple that had built it, and speculating about how many other Tyndallites might have their lawns maintained by anyone other than themselves, let alone a landscaper from thirty miles away. After watching the guy make a couple of passes back and forth across the lawn, I shook my head at the sight and decided that it was well past time for a beer.

I dropped the Chrysler into gear and headed on over to the Dugout. Walking through the door, I saw that the two women from Tuesday night were back at the bar, along with the elderly couple that had been there on my first night in town. Happily, Mack, the heating and air-conditioning guy, did not appear to be in attendance.

I took a seat at the end of the bar, leaving two stools between me and the women, who appeared to be drinking Chablis again. No one was behind the bar, but the blond offered a smile and said, "Matt had to go out back for a minute, but he should be here momentarily. You could probably just help yourself to a beer until he gets back."

The words were barely out of her mouth, though, when Matt emerged from the kitchen and said hello. He set me up with an MGD and asked me how my day had gone. "Reasonably well," I said. "How's yours?"

"Pretty good. I hear somebody took a shot at you last night."

Before I could reply, the brunette slammed her glass down on the bar and said, "Holy shit! Somebody tried to kill you?"

I waved her off. "No—at least I don't think so. The sheriff suspects that it was just somebody who got liquored up and decided to take a shot at a passing car. I doubt that whoever did it was aiming at me personally, let alone trying to kill me."

The woman picked up her drink again and took a healthy sip. "Boy, there are some weird assholes out there, that's for sure."

She went quiet for a moment and Matt said, "Did you connect with Sarah Paine?"

"I did, thanks. And I had a nice conversation with her father out at the assisted living center. He was a big help. Speaking of which, do you know anybody around here with the last names Howard or Checka—or maybe a daughter or a granddaughter of a man by that name who might still be living here but with a different last name like Sarah Grimke Paine?"

The bartender thought about it for a moment, then shook his head. "Nope, neither name rings a bell."

The blonde Chablis drinker scrunched her face up in concentration and then said, "Not with me neither."

Throughout the conversation up to that point, the elderly couple at the other end of the bar had sat quietly, drinking their Budweisers, and apparently tuning out everything around them. But then the woman, who appeared to be in her early seventies, set down her bottle, leaned around her husband and said, "Well, there is Millie Hopworth. She's the granddaughter of the guy who was the sheriff here back in the 1930s."

I leaned forward, looked down the bar to the woman and said, "Does she still live here in town, Ma'am?"

She nodded. "Over on Eleventh Avenue. Her husband, Bob, passed about eight years ago, but she's still in the same house where they lived."

"Would she be in the phone book?"

"Oh, sure. I'd imagine so."

Before I could ask, Matt turned, grabbed a phone book, and set it on the bar in front of me. Flipping through the pages of the small volume, I tried to remember the last time I'd actually used a phone book. I found the H's and ran my finger down the column to the listing for "Hopworth, Robert." It listed a phone number and an address at 113 Eleventh Avenue. Holding the spot, I walked down to the other end of the bar and showed the listing to the woman. "Is that it?"

"That's her," she replied.

I borrowed a pad of paper and a pen from Matt and made a note of the name, address and phone number. I thanked the woman for her help and offered to pay for their beers. I paid for my own at the same time, finished the last of it, and headed on back to the Welcome Inn.

24.

Back at the motel, I sat down on the bed and punched Mrs. Hopworth's number into my phone. It rang four times before a woman who sounded fairly elderly offered a tentative "hello?" and confirmed that she was Millie Hopworth.

"Mrs. Hopworth," I said, "my name is Jack Oliva. I'm a retired police detective from Phoenix and I'm up here doing some research into my family's history. They used to live here in Tyndall until the middle 1930s. While doing my research, I came across the name of Sheriff Gary Checka who I understand was your grandfather."

"That's right."

"I was wondering, if it's not too much trouble, if I might be able to come by tomorrow and talk to you a bit about your grandfather, maybe some time in the late morning or early afternoon?"

"Well, I have a doctor's appointment at one o'clock over in Tabor, and I'll have to leave for that at around noon. But if you wanted to come by around eleven or so, I could talk to you then."

"That would be fine Ma'am, and I really appreciate the opportunity to meet you. I'll look forward to seeing you then."

* * *

I waited for Mrs. Hopworth to break the connection and then decided to take a shower before I headed out to dinner. Twenty minutes later, I locked my computer bag in the trunk again and pointed the Chrysler north up the street.

As had been the case on the three previous nights, the café was doing a reasonably good dinnertime business. I took an empty booth about midway down the line and ordered another Chicken-

Fried Steak from the young waitress. I followed that with a piece of cherry pie, which turned out to be just as delicious as the others I'd tried. I told the waitress to be sure and extend my compliments to her aunt and then decided to take a walk, in hopes of burning up some of the calories I'd just consumed.

It was another very nice evening and so I walked north up Main Street a couple of blocks and then headed west in the direction of the city park. Three small children were playing on the swings and a woman whom I assumed was their mother was sitting on a nearby bench, keeping an eye on the kids while at the same time texting a message into her phone. A couple of elderly people were walking slowly on the pathway that looped around the lake, and I dropped in behind them. I made two circuits of the lake and then walked back to my car and turned south down the street, back toward the motel.

A block and a half later, my buddy in the Honda from earlier in the day passed me going in the other direction. He was studiously watching the street ahead of him and appeared to take no notice of me. At the motel, I pulled into the drive and parked in front of my unit. I grabbed my computer bag from the trunk and went to open the door to my room, only to realize that it was already open. Someone had used a tool of some sort to jimmy the door at the point where the lock met the jamb and the door was now standing open a couple of inches.

The blinds in the room were still closed, just the way I'd left them, and I had no way of knowing whether someone might still be in the room. I slipped back to the car, raised the trunk lid as quietly as I could, put my computer bag back in the trunk, then closed the lid again.

Quickly scanning the area, I saw no one else around, let alone anyone who might have been paying any attention to me. I pulled the pistol out my ankle holster and jacked a round into the chamber. Back at the door to the room, I pressed myself flat against the wall on the far side of the doorknob and listened for the sounds of any activity coming from the room. Hearing nothing, I took a deep breath and then leaned over and pushed the door open.

Nothing happened.

The door swung wide open, but I still heard nothing from the room. Moving quickly now, I stepped into the room, sweeping it with the gun. The bedding had been pulled off the mattress and my suitcase was lying open, empty on top of the bed. The dresser drawers had all been pulled open and my clothing was scattered all over the place.

The door to the closet was standing open and the clothes I'd hung there had all been pushed aside. Other than the clothes, though, the closet was empty, leaving only the small bathroom as a possible hiding place. Still holding the Glock out in front of me, I moved quietly across the room and waited for a couple of seconds near the bathroom door, which was also standing open. Hearing nothing, I spun quickly into the doorway, but the room was empty.

The only things I'd left in the room were my clothes, my toiletries, and the novel I was reading, and nothing seemed to be missing. Perhaps someone had broken in, hoping that I'd left cash or some valuables in the room, but that seemed unlikely, especially when combined with the fact that someone had taken a shot at me less than twenty-four hours earlier. My immediate conclusion, then, was that someone had broken in looking for my computer and for any notes I might have taken. Fortunately, everything of any value, including the research I had done, was safely in the computer bag in the trunk of the Chrysler, and on the flash drive I was using as a backup, which was in my pocket.

I couldn't believe that Alex Benson would have felt threatened enough by my actions or that Mack, the heating and air-conditioning guy, would have been angry enough by my presence in town to have done something like this. There was, of course, the kid in the Honda who I'd passed on the street only a few minutes before I got back to the motel, but what the hell was his story?

Sighing heavily, I returned the Glock to the trunk, pulled out my phone and called the sheriff's office again.

* * *

The dispatcher at the sheriff's office patched me through to Stan Davis who was out on patrol. It occurred to me that the guy seemed to spend virtually all of his time on duty, and I wondered if that might be because his office was understaffed or if it was because he simply enjoyed the work. He told me that he would be there in ten, and I went back outside and waited for him, leaving the room exactly as I'd found it.

Davis arrived fairly quickly and pulled up next to my Chrysler. The motel manager was outside watering some plants in front of the office and, no doubt curious about what the sheriff might be doing at his motel, the guy set down his watering can and headed in our direction. He nodded at me, greeted the sheriff and asked Davis if there was a problem.

"Apparently so, Milt." Pointing at the damaged door to my unit, he said, "Looks like someone broke into Mr. Oliva's room here."

The manager turned to look at the door and then to me. "Oh, dear. Is there anything missing?"

"No. Whoever it was went through my things pretty thoroughly, but as far as I can tell, they didn't take anything and they didn't do any damage to the room, save for prying open the door."

Davis turned to me and said, "When do you think it happened?"

"Everything was fine when I left to go to dinner about six thirty. I got back a little after eight and found the door jimmied open.

Whoever it was had left by then, so I imagine they broke in sometime between six-thirty and seven thirty or maybe seven forty-five at the outside."

Davis nodded. "You see any suspicious looking characters around about then, Milt?"

"No, Sheriff. Laura and I sat down to dinner about six fifteen, and I was back in the residence until a couple of minutes ago when I came out to do some watering. From back there, of course, I can't see the front of the motel."

"Anybody been hanging around in the last day or so, looking like they might be casing the place?"

The manager shook his head.

"And I take it that no one came in and asked which room Mr. Oliva might be in?"

"No, Sheriff."

Davis nodded. "Well, they wouldn't have had to do that, I don't suppose." Turning to me, he continued, "Since your car is always parked right outside your front door when you're in the room, it wouldn't take a genius to figure out which unit you were in."

"No, I wouldn't think so."

"Well, let's go in and take a look."

Davis led the way into the unit, and I followed with the manager trailing behind. The sheriff walked through, checking the condition of the room without saying anything. Finally, he turned and said, "You're sure nothing is missing?"

I shook my head. "Unless the guy stole a pair of socks or something that I'm not noticing in the moment, everything I left in the room appears to still be here. I didn't leave any valuables here and so if it was someone looking for cash or jewelry or something like that, they were out of luck."

"What else could they have been looking for, Jack?"

I took a quick glance at the motel manager and shrugged. "Nothing I can think of, Sheriff."

Davis paused for a moment and then turned to the manager. "What that broken door, Milt, Mr. Oliva will be needing another room for tonight. Do you want to go back and do the paperwork? Mr. Oliva can pick up the key once we're done here and move his things to the new room."

"Of course, Sheriff."

We watched as the manager walked back to the office and then Davis turned back to me. "You were saying, Jack?"

"I really didn't think that this was a conversation we needed to have in front of the manager, Sheriff, but the only thing I can think of that somebody might have been looking for would be the notes on my research. I can't imagine why anyone would be interested in any of that, and normally, I'd simply assume that this was the act of a thief looking to score cash or something he could pawn. But when you add in the fact that somebody left me a warning note at the library yesterday and combine that with the fact that someone took a shot at me last night, and I'm beginning to wonder if someone doesn't feel threatened by my presence up here for some reason that I can't possibly begin to divine.

"In addition, of course there was the kid who was following me earlier in the day. Coincidentally, I passed him on the street going in the other direction as I was coming back here thirty minutes ago. And, on top of all that, I had a very strange encounter with Alex Benson this afternoon."

"Strange how?"

"I was working in the library and he came in, sat down at the table, and accused me of poking into his family's business. I explained that I wasn't really interested in his family, but that I was curious about the relationship between my grandfather and his great-grandfather. The two of them worked together at the bank before my grandfather shot himself.

"Benson then said that someone had told him that I had accused his great-grandfather of being complicit in my grandfather's crime. I told him that was absolutely untrue and that I'd never even suspected such a thing, let alone said it to anyone else. He warned me to mind my own business and to leave his family alone. He told me that he was a hugely important man in this community and that he could make my life very difficult if he wanted to."

Davis snorted. "Did you believe him?"

"Up to a point. I'm sure that his company is important enough to the economy of this town that some people would bend over backwards to keep him happy. That said, I'm a pretty good judge of character, Sheriff, and you don't strike me as a person who'd be carrying water for a guy the likes of Alex Benson."

The sheriff shook his head. "Not hardly." He paused for a second, then said, "I ran the plate on the car that was following you. It belongs to a punk named Johnny Holloway. He's had a few run-ins with my department, speeding in that piece-of-shit Honda that he drives, and a drunk-and-disorderly that cost him a pretty stiff fine and a weekend in residence with us. He's worked here and there, never for very long, but he did work for a year or so as a general flunky at Benson's company."

"Interesting."

"Yeah," Davis said, "but I don't know that we could make anything out of it."

Looking back toward my room he said, "As I'm sure you've already noticed, there are no video cameras here at the motel or anywhere along the street that might give us a look at your perpetrator. I could get a detective to come down here and process the scene, but I doubt that he'd come up with anything useful."

"I doubt it too, Sheriff, and I don't see the point in wasting your detective's time or your other resources on it. Maybe if I'd gotten back here a bit earlier..."

"Maybe, Jack.... Tell you what; I think I'll have one of my deputies pick up Holloway and bring him in for a little discussion on the grounds that he was harassing a visitor to our community. I'll ask him why he was following you, and of course, he'll tell me that he wasn't. I'll ask why he was seen driving away from the motel just after your room was burglarized, and of course, he'll insist that he wasn't anywhere near your room. Then I'll tell him that I'm issuing an informal restraining order and that if I hear that he's been seen anywhere near you again between now and the time you leave, I'll be throwing his ass in the can."

"I appreciate it, Sheriff, but I wish to hell I could figure out what's going on here."

"So do I, Jack. You just keep your eyes open and be careful out there.

25.

Davis got back into his Jeep, and I watched him drive away. As he did, the motel manager returned, bringing me the key to a room two doors down from the one that had been broken into. I took the key, thanked him, and apologized for the problem. "Don't worry," he said. "It's hardly your fault that somebody broke in and threw your things all over the room."

"Just out of curiosity, has anything like this ever happened here before?"

"Not really. Five or six years ago, we had some kids break out a window in the back and sneak into a room in the middle of the night. From what they left behind, they were using the room for drinking beer and having sex. But they were long gone by the time I noticed the broken window the next morning, and I never figured out who it might have been."

"Well, again, I'm sorry," I said. "I'll quickly move my stuff to the other room, and if you like, I'll help you secure that door so that it stays closed overnight."

"That's okay. Once you've finished moving into the other room, I'll just put a nail in the door to hold it until I can fix it in the morning."

*　*　*

I quickly gathered up my things and moved them into the new room. I decided, though, to leave my car parked where it was, on the off chance that someone was using it as a marker to determine which room I was in. I grabbed my computer bag and the Glock from the trunk and set the gun on the nightstand next to the bed, just in case I had another surprise visitor during the night. Then I poured myself a generous helping of Elmer T. Lee and dropped onto the bed, trying to figure out what in the hell was going on here.

I no longer believed that someone had taken a potshot at a passing car last night and had just happened to hit mine. And I certainly didn't believe that I'd been the victim of a random burglary tonight. I also didn't believe that Johnny Holloway, whoever in the hell he was, would have decided to follow me for reasons of his own. Someone had put him up to it, but who and why?

And what the hell was up with Alex Benson? Did he really believe that I was besmirching his family's good name? Had someone really told him that I believed that his great-grandfather had been complicit in my grandfather's crime? Who could have told him that, and why? And could Benson possibly think that there might be any truth in the accusation?

Even if his great-grandfather had been my grandfather's accomplice, I doubt that he would have admitted it to anyone, and I certainly couldn't imagine that the story would have been passed along through the generations to his great-grandson.

The fact that Holloway had worked for Benson, even if only briefly, suggested that Benson might well be the person who had put Holloway on my trail. Having heard that I was "poking into his family's business," perhaps he had told Holloway to follow me and report my activities back to him. But had Benson also sent me the anonymous threat?

For lack of a better suspect, and given the fact that I *had* seen him in the vicinity of the motel just before I discovered the burglary, Holloway was my most likely candidate for the person who had broken into my room. I assumed that he must have been looking for my computer and/or my research notes. But what did Benson, or whomever, think might be in those notes?

Maybe the guy was just paranoid. Or maybe there *was* something out there that clearly threatened him—or someone—and

I just hadn't found it yet. Or perhaps I *had* found it but simply hadn't recognized it for what it was.

With that thought turning over in my mind, I finished the whiskey and checked my watch. It was now nine thirty in South Dakota, which meant it was seven thirty in Phoenix and that Annie should have had time to get home from work and have her dinner. I grabbed my cell phone from the nightstand and speed-dialed her phone. A moment later, she connected to the call and said, "I was just thinking about you."

"Something nice, I hope."

"Always, and in this case, something *particularly* nice. I really wish you were here, Jack."

"I wish I was too, Hon. I'd especially like to be with you right at the moment."

"Me too. So, how's your research going?"

I decided on the spur of the moment not to mention the problems I'd encountered for fear of possibly upsetting her, so I took a deep breath and said, "Pretty well, actually. I've filled in a lot of the blanks about the events surrounding my grandfather's death and the subsequent failure of the bank, which, it appears, really was a disaster for this little town back then. People here were already being hammered by the agricultural depression and the last thing they needed was for one of their two local banks to go under. Then, to add insult to injury, the town's only other bank failed a few years later."

"And their deposits weren't insured?"

"Not yet. This was still a few years before the federal government began insuring banking deposits."

"I'll bet that was grim then."

"Absolutely. So how was your day?"

"Not bad. Work was okay, and after I met my friend Susan at The Mission for Happy Hour. I had chips and salsa and a couple of margaritas for dinner, and so, other than being very lonely for you, I'm feeling pretty good at the moment."

"Well, I'm really looking forward to addressing that loneliness problem in only forty-eight hours or so."

"Me too, Jack. Will you call me again tomorrow?"

"Of course."

"I'll look forward to that too. Hey, Jack?"

"Yeah?"

"I love you."

I hesitated for a second, caught up in the emotion of the unexpected moment, then said, "I love you too, Annie."

"Promise you'll come back to me soon and safely."

"I promise, Hon."

We ended the call and I set my phone back on the nightstand, wondering about the implications of the way our conversation had ended. My declaration had not been a reflexive response to Annie's; I knew that I *did* love her, even if I hadn't ventured to say it out loud until just now, either to her or to myself. But would the fact that we had both now taken that step affect our relationship going forward, and if so, how?

Truth to tell, I was very comfortable with things the way they were, and I thought that Annie was too. But were her hopes and expectations now changing? Would she now want a more serious commitment? And how would I react if she did? My track record in the relationship department was not all that great, and I did not want to disappoint Annie. God knows, I certainly didn't want to lose her, and I hoped that, moving forward, our relationship would continue to grow and improve and would not suffer the kinds of problems that had plagued my earlier ones.

But perhaps I was overthinking the situation, as I have often been wont to do. Perhaps Annie was just finally expressing an emotion that she'd felt for a while now and was not anticipating any significant change in our relationship. Whatever the case, I guessed that I'd find out soon enough, and on that note, I crawled into bed, wondering what Friday might bring.

26.

I read a few chapters of the Virgil Flowers novel, then turned the light off a little before eleven and dropped almost immediately into a deep sleep. I had no idea how long I'd been sleeping when I was awakened by the sound of someone knocking on the door of my room. I rolled slowly out of bed without turning on any lights and stepped over to the window, noting that the digital clock on the small nightstand next to the bed read 2:28 a.m.

I lifted one of the blinds fronting the window just far enough to see the sheriff's jeep parked in the motel driveway alongside my Chrysler. I stepped over to the door and said, "Sheriff?"

"Yeah, it's me, Jack."

"Give me a minute; I'll be right with you."

I flipped on the light, pulled on a tee shirt and my jeans, and then grabbed my pistol which was lying on the nightstand and slipped it underneath the mattress. Then I unlocked the door and opened it to find the sheriff and one of his young deputies standing on the porch. I stepped aside to let them into the room and said, "What's happened, Sheriff?"

The two men stepped into the small room and made a quick appraisal of the surroundings, the sheriff looking like he might have just gotten out of bed himself. He pushed his hat back a bit, then looked at me and said, "Can I ask how you've spent the evening since I last saw you, Jack?"

I shrugged. "I haven't left the motel since then, Sheriff. I moved my things down to this room from the old one, and once I was settled in, I spent a few minutes on the phone with my girlfriend down in Phoenix. I crawled into bed with the book I'm reading and then turned out the lights a little after eleven. I fell to sleep pretty quickly and was still sleeping when you woke me up."

"I see you didn't move your car."

"No. As you pointed out before, it's at least possible that whoever broke into my room earlier was using the car to pinpoint which room I was in. I decided to leave it in front of the old room in case whoever it was decided to make a return visit."

"When was the last time you saw Alex Benson?"

"The last time I saw him—and the *only* time I've ever seen him—was this afternoon at the library."

"You didn't see him when you drove out to his house at five fourteen this afternoon and sat out front of the place for two minutes and forty-three seconds before driving off?"

"No, I didn't, Sheriff, and I have no idea if he was even home at the time. I gather that he must have video surveillance monitoring the front of his house."

"Yup. You wanna tell me why you were cruising the place, Jack?"

"Just curious. Tracy, the librarian, offered the observation that Benson had built a house that was totally inappropriate for Tyndall and I decided to take a look for myself."

"And?"

"And she was right. The place is totally out of character for the neighborhood and for the town as well, for that matter. What's happened to Benson?"

"Someone smacked him a good one on the back of the head when he was coming home about one o'clock this morning."

"And you think it might have been me who did it?"

"Well, I have to wonder. You have a confrontation with the guy at the library. A couple of hours later the video catches you casing the guy's house, and seven hours after that, somebody whacks him over the head."

"Well, Sheriff, as I'm sure the librarian will tell you, Benson confronted *me* at the library; I didn't confront him. And, as I told you earlier, *he* was the one who threatened me, and not the other way around. If someone had assaulted me tonight, he might be a logical suspect, but why would I want to assault him—what's the motive here?"

"Damned if I know, Jack. But you know I've got to talk to you about it."

"Of course. What's his condition, by the way?"

"He'll live, but he's gonna have a helluva headache for the next few days."

"And what does the video show?"

"It shows Benson pulling up to the gates in front of his driveway at one-oh-two in the morning. The gates don't open when he apparently pushes the button on his remote and so he gets out of the car to see what's wrong. Turns out that somebody jammed a steel rod into the mechanism that prevented the gates from working.

"Anyhow, Benson's standing there looking at the damned thing when somebody slips up behind him and cracks him on the right side of the head with a short piece of pipe or some such thing. Then Benson falls to the ground and the assailant quickly picks through his pockets. He takes Benson's watch and wallet but leaves his phone. Then he runs off into the night."

"No vehicle visible?"

"No."

"And it's impossible to identify the assailant from the video."

"Right. The guy is dressed all in dark clothing including gloves and a hoodie that's tied up tight around his face. And, of course, Benson never got a look at him."

"And you thought that even though I knew that the temperature and the humidity were both going to be in the mid-nineties up here, I still packed my black hoodie and my gloves just on the off chance that I might have to attack somebody in the middle of the night while I was here?"

"Did you?"

"Of course not. But feel free to take a look through my clothes as long as you're here."

The sheriff shook his head. "Probably no need to do that. If you had attacked Benson, you would have been smart enough to get rid of the gloves and the hoodie."

"I'd certainly hope so, Sheriff. So, tell me, what in the hell was Alex Benson doing coming home at one o'clock in the morning? This doesn't strike me as a town where the nightlife goes on quite that late."

"Benson plays in a big poker game down in Yankton on Thursday nights. He was coming home from the game."

"How'd he do?"

"I don't know yet. What does that matter?"

"I was just wondering if he might have been a big winner. Maybe someone who got busted out of the game early decided to come up here and wait for Benson to get home in the hope of getting his money back. Or, in the alternative, if it's fairly common knowledge that Benson plays in this game, maybe someone else decided to hope that he was coming home a winner tonight and tried to cash in."

The sheriff nodded. "Both possibilities, I suppose. Or it might just be that someone was pissed off at him for some totally unrelated reason—a disgruntled employee or customer or whatever. Benson has always had something of a talent for antagonizing people."

So, Sheriff, where does that leave us?"

"Probably nowhere, Jack, but do you mind if we take a look in your car?"

"Be my guest."

I grabbed the key fob for the Chrysler from the top of the desk and hit the buttons to unlock the door and pop the trunk. Then I slipped into my shoes and followed the sheriff and his deputy out to the car. The sheriff opened the driver's door while the deputy opened the rear door behind it. The deputy looked into the car and then said, "Sheriff?"

The sheriff moved around the deputy and leaned over to look into the back seat. Then he raised up again, turned to face me and said, "What do we have here, Jack?"

I stepped over and looked into the back seat. Lying in the middle of the seat was a wooden club, perhaps twenty-four inches long, that was tapered something on the order of a small baseball bat. A few dark specks that might have been blood stained the business end of the thing.

Turning back, I shook my head. "I have no idea Sheriff. I've never seen it before."

"And yet it's sitting in the back seat of your locked-up rental car."

"Locked-up being a relative description in this case, Sheriff. Obviously, anyone could have pulled the tape and the plastic sheeting back a bit from the rear window there, slipped that thing through the opening and then taped it up again. You wouldn't really need to be a genius with a set of lock picks to have gotten into the car.

"That said, assuming that is the weapon with which Benson was attacked, it would seem to throw most of our earlier theories out the window. Hard to imagine that a losing poker player from Yankton or one of Benson's disgruntled employees would even know that I was here in town, let alone know what sort of car I'd be driving or where it might be parked so they could plant that bat in the back seat and put me in the frame."

"Obviously."

"Of course you'd also have to wonder why, if I was so careful to get rid of the gloves and the hoodie I was wearing when I attacked Benson, I'd be so fucking stupid as to leave the bat I hit him with lying in plain view on the back seat of my rental car."

"Yeah, you would at that, Jack. So, who do you suppose might want to put you in the frame for something like this?"

"You're guess is as good as mine, Sheriff Davis. Maybe the person who sent me the note at the library, or maybe the person who took a shot at me the other night, assuming that they're not one and the same person, decided to amp up the pressure when I wasn't immediately scared into leaving town. Maybe the person who broke into my room tonight didn't find what he was looking for and decided to come at me from another angle. The only thing that *doesn't* make any sense is the idea that I would have attacked Alex Benson. Again, what the hell would my motive have been? I don't even know the guy and as I told you earlier, I certainly didn't take his threats against me seriously."

Davis sighed and shook his head, looking like a man who really wished that he were back home in bed. Turning to the deputy, he said, "Put on some gloves and bag that thing, Willie. We'll send it off to the lab to make sure that's Benson's blood on it and on the off chance that someone was dumb enough to leave fingerprints on it."

Looking earnestly at the sheriff, the deputy said, "And do you want me to cuff the suspect, sir?"

Davis looked to me, rolled his eyes, and then looked back at the deputy. "Not tonight, Willie. We'll maybe save that until sometime tomorrow, depending on how things go."

Turning back to me, he said, "You're not going to suddenly leave town, are you, Jack?"

"Not until Saturday, Sheriff."

"Well, be sure to check with me before you do, that is unless I find some reason to come back and talk to you later tonight or tomorrow."

I watched as the young deputy carefully gloved up, then retrieved the bat and dropped it into an evidence bag. That done, he closed the car doors and the sheriff touched the brim of his hat. "Sleep well, Jack," he said. Then he and the deputy got back into the jeep and rolled slowly down the driveway and back out to the street.

27.

As Alice had once famously observed on arriving in Wonderland, things were getting curiouser and curiouser.

I undressed again, turned out the lights and crawled back into bed, wondering who in the hell might have assaulted Alex Benson and why they would have attempted to pin the attack on me. I assumed that the bat that the deputy had found in the back seat of my car was almost certainly the weapon that had been used to assault Benson. And given that someone had gone to all the trouble of planting it in my car, it also seemed logical to assume that the ultimate purpose of the attack was to get me entangled with the law and possibly charged with assault or something worse. In that event, Benson would have become caught up in the action only because of our argument in the library and not because someone actually had a specific grievance against him.

I'd earlier assumed that Johnny Holloway, the kid who had been following me, and whom I also assumed was the likeliest person to have broken into my room, was working for Benson. But if that were true, certainly he would not have attacked Benson. Was it possible that Holloway was working for someone else and that he'd been ordered to attack Benson and then slip the weapon into my car? But if so why, and who was giving the orders?

And if Holloway was not involved in the attack, then who was? If he had not planted the bat in my car, then who had?

I lay awake for a couple of hours or so, tossing and turning, and running the various permutations of the problem through my mind without coming up with any solution that seemed remotely viable. I finally fell back to sleep and woke up at seven thirty on

Friday morning, still thinking about the attack on Alex Benson and feeling guilty about the fact that I hadn't gotten any real exercise in almost a week. My appointment with Anna Nelson at the Heritage Museum wasn't for another couple of hours yet, and so I dragged myself out of bed, used the bathroom, and then pulled on a tee shirt, a pair of shorts, and my running shoes.

I put my backup flash drive in the pocket of the shorts, along with my room key and the key to the Chrysler. I locked the Glock and my computer bag in the trunk, hoping that whoever had broken into my room wouldn't think to jimmy the trunk open next. I felt a little naked without the pistol, but there was simply no way to wear it without being completely obvious about it, and so I decided to leave it in the car, hoping that the bad guys in and around Tyndall, South Dakota didn't get up any earlier than the bad guys in most other places.

It was a beautiful sunny morning, with the temperature somewhere in the low seventies. Fortunately, the humidity was not too bad and so I set off south down the street, running slowly at first until I was reasonably well warmed up. A couple of blocks later, I turned left onto Tenth Avenue, preferring to run on the quieter residential streets, rather than through the business district.

For the first mile or so, my body gave me a little grief about the fact that I hadn't done this for several days, but I gradually worked out the kinks and picked up the pace. As had been the case since I first arrived, the town seemed eerily quiet, even for this time of the morning. I saw only a couple of cars out on the street, and I didn't see anyone else out walking or running, or even working out in their yards. On the plus side, though, no one pulled out a gun and took a shot at me. Fifteen minutes out, I reversed course and ran back to the motel. I got there twenty-eight minutes after leaving and figured that I'd run three and a half to four miles, which was good enough for today.

It appeared that no one had bothered either the car or my room in my absence, but as I was slipping the key into the door, the sheriff's Jeep pulled up the long driveway and stopped behind my Chrysler. The sheriff dragged himself out of the Jeep looking like he hadn't gotten back to bed since our conversation several hours earlier. He looked at me, standing on the porch in my running gear, then shook his head and said, "Christ, Jack, you got enough sleep last night to have the energy to go out running?"

"What can I say, Sheriff; I woke up an hour or so ago and couldn't sleep any more. I thought a run might help me to think more clearly."

"And did it?"

"Not so's you'd notice, I'm afraid to say."

We settled into a couple of chairs on the porch. Davis took off his hat and turned it slowly through his hands. "I hate to sound like a cliched western movie, Jack, but until you rode into Tyndall, this was a peaceful, quiet little town. And since you got here, it seems like we've had nothing but trouble."

"I'm genuinely sorry about that, Sheriff, and I wish to hell that I had some idea why all this is happening. But I just can't for the life of me figure out why my looking into what happened to my mom's family's up here a hundred years ago would have pissed somebody off or made them feel threatened in some way. It just makes no damned sense at all. Can I ask if you've talked to that Johnny Holloway kid?"

"Not yet, why?"

"He's the only thread, thin as it is, that seems to be constant through this. For some reason, he was following me around town. Then I saw him driving north a couple of blocks away from the motel here just before I discovered that my room had been broken into.

"After you told me that he was something of a lowlife and that he used to work for Alex Benson, I was sort of assuming that

Benson had probably hired him, first to follow me and then to break into my room, looking for my research notes or something. But now that Benson's been attacked, I find myself wondering if someone else might be pulling the strings and if they also ordered Holloway to attack Benson and then slip the weapon into my car."

"It's a thought. We'll grab him up and have a chat with him first thing this morning."

"When do you think you'll get the results of the lab work on that bat you found in my car last night?"

"Not soon enough, of course. We'll get it over to the state crime lab in Pierre today, but it will doubtless be several days at least before we get a response."

I brushed away a fly that was now intent on buzzing my forehead and said, "Assuming that it proves to be the weapon, it seems clear to me that someone attacked Benson and then put the bat in my car as a way of getting me tangled up with the law. It also seems logical to assume that the person who planned this out must have known that Benson threatened me in the library yesterday. Otherwise, why would an attack on Benson lead you to look at me?"

"Okay, I'll buy that."

"I told no one about the incident except for you. Tracy, the librarian witnessed it, but I can't imagine that she's masterminding all this business. It's possible, I suppose, that she quite innocently mentioned it to the person who is. Otherwise, the mastermind has to be someone that Benson told about our conversation. Did he go bragging to the wrong person that he'd put the fear of God into me or some such thing?

"Whichever the case, the only suggestion I have is that, in addition to sweating Holloway, you interview both the librarian and Benson and find out who, if anyone, they talked to about all of this."

Looking over at him, I shook my head and said, "Before you do that, though, I'd suggest that you go home and catch a few hours in the sack. You look like you're about to fall asleep in that chair."

"No shit. I feel like I could sleep for a month. But as you know full well, in a case like this, you've got to keep moving early on. Otherwise you lose the momentum and your chances of solving the damned thing begin to evaporate."

"I do know that, Sheriff. I only wish I could do something to help."

"I do too, Jack. If you think of anything else, let me know. And as I said last night, you need to be watching your back. There's somebody out there who's enormously pissed at you, and the fact that you're not in jail this morning may cause whoever it is to take another shot at you sooner rather than later."

28.

I watched the sheriff drive off in the direction of his office, then I retrieved the Glock and my computer bag from the trunk, let myself into the room and took a long, hot shower. I took my time getting ready, and a couple minutes after nine, I settled onto a stool at the counter in the café. Meg put a cup of coffee in front of me and we chatted for a couple of minutes while I waited for the coffee to cool a bit. Meg then left to deliver an order to another customer, and I was just preparing to take a sip of the coffee when somebody placed a hand on my shoulder. I turned to see my cousin standing behind me. "Hey, Jack," he said, sticking out his hand.

We shook hands and I said, "Good to see you, Bud, how's things?"

"Well, they're fine with me, but I hear that you had some excitement after you left our place the other night."

"A bit."

"I'm sitting over here at a table by myself; why don't you grab your cup and join me?"

I picked up coffee and followed him over to a two-top by the window. Pointing at my coffee, he said, "That's your idea of breakfast?"

"I've never been much of a breakfast guy. My whole life, food has never really looked all that good to me much before noon."

My cousin settled into his chair behind a breakfast that consisted of orange juice, coffee, a couple of eggs, a slice of ham, and hash-browned potatoes. Laughing, he said, "I envy you that. I can't function unless I've got a full meal in me first thing in the morning." Slapping his stomach, he said, "Of course that probably accounts for the fact that I'm carrying this gut around while you look to be in perfect shape."

"I'd think that you'd be doing enough hard work out there on your farm that you'd easily burn up any excess calories you might be consuming."

"Well, that certainly would have been true back in the old days. But now everything I do is so mechanized and computerized that I probably don't get as much exercise as you used to get when you were still chasing bad guys around Phoenix."

"Do you normally eat breakfast here in town?" I asked.

"No. Becky usually fixes breakfast for us at home, but she's visiting her mom up in Minot this weekend, so I'm on my own. I had to get to the post office and run a few other errands this morning, and so I thought I'd stop in and grab some breakfast while I was here. So, tell me, what the hell happened the other night anyway?

I shook my head. "I really don't know, Bud. I was a couple of miles outside of town, taking my time driving back in the dark, and all of a sudden, I heard a shot and the window behind me exploded. I got the hell back to town as fast as I could and reported it to the sheriff. He says that somebody fired the shot from a soybean field, but there's no way of knowing who it might have been, or if they were really aiming at me. The sheriff thinks it might have just been some drunk who decided to take a shot at a passing car."

Bud grunted. "That sounds like a stretch to me. What would some drunk be doing wandering around in a soybean field at ten o'clock on a Wednesday night, let alone with a gun? And why in the hell would he decide to take a shot at a passing car just for the fun of it?"

I shrugged. "Who the hell knows? The only other alternative is that somebody knew that I'd be driving along that road and set up in that field for the express purpose of taking a shot at me."

"Well, shit, that sounds like a stretch too. I mean who in the hell would be mad at you for any reason, let alone mad enough to take a shot at you?"

I threw up my hands. "Search me. I ran into a guy at the Dugout the other night who knew that my grandfather had caused the bank to fail back in 1925 and who was still pissed off about it. He claims it ruined his grandfather's life, his father's life, and his as well. Maybe there's somebody else out there who feels the same way and decided to even the score or some damned thing."

My cousin shook his head. "That would be some pretty weird shit." He paused long enough to drain the last of his coffee, then said, "So how's your research coming?"

I fluttered my hand. "So, so. I'm getting a reasonably good feel for what the town was like back then and for what the ramifications of my grandfather's actions turned out to be, both for the town and for his family. I've seen the house where they lived, and I've seen the place where he died, and that pretty much accomplishes everything I hoped to do by coming up here. What's nagging at me though, is that I still have no idea why in the hell he stole all that money or what in God's name he did with it."

"I understand, but I don't know how you'd ever figure that out at this late date."

"I know, but it's still bugging the hell out of me. It's the one unresolved piece of this whole damned puzzle."

He set his coffee cup back on the table. "Changing the subject, I know tonight's your last night in town. What with Becky being away, I'm on my own. Why don't you come on out for dinner? We can drink some beer and I'll throw a couple of giant steaks on the grill."

"Thanks, Bud. I'd enjoy that, if you're sure it won't be a problem."

"None at all. That's what I'd be doing for dinner anyway, and I'd really enjoy your company. Why don't you come out about six again?"

"I'll look forward to it. Thanks, Bud"

* * *

Bud left to run his errands before heading back out to the farm and I finished my coffee and settled up with Meg. Then I went out to the Chrysler and headed down the street to the museum. It was a small, one-story yellow clapboard building set off the street on a large lot next to a small white church with a sign identifying it as "Bon Homme Memorial Church 1885." A light blue Volkswagen Bug was parked in front of the museum, and I assumed that it probably belonged to Anna Nelson.

I parked behind the Bug and walked up to the door. Just as I raised my hand to knock, the door opened, and I found myself looking at a petite redhead who appeared to be somewhere in her middle fifties. She was dressed in a pair of tan shorts and a blue tee-shirt. Wire-rimmed glasses rested on a small, upturned nose and fronted hazel eyes. "You must be Mr. Oliva," she said.

"Guilty. And you must be Ms. Nelson."

"Anna," she said, offering her hand.

We shook hands and she led me into the building, which appeared to consist of one large room with a restroom off to the side. A number of items were displayed on tables around the room, and the walls were filled with framed pictures and documents. As I took in the scene, Nelson said, "I understand that you're up here researching your family's history."

"That's right. My mother was born here in 1919 and lived here until she and my grandmother moved to Montana in the middle 1930s."

"And your grandfather was Charles Kratina?"

"Correct. I've spent the last couple of afternoons up the street in the library reading through the newspapers from the 1920s and

'30s, getting a general sense of the town back then and looking for information about my grandfather and the problems at the bank. I've also looked at the community histories they have up there, and I was hoping that you might have some materials here that would bear on all of that."

Nelson shook her head. "I'm sorry to say that I'm probably not going to be of much help. We don't really have a document collection here—no newspapers or letter collections or anything like that. We do have copies of the community histories that you've probably already seen at the library, and we do have a collection of photos.

"We have some diaries of old homesteaders and things like that, but I'm sure that nothing in there would be of much use to you. You might find some of your family members in the picture collection, though."

"That would be good; I've only ever seen a couple of pictures of my grandfather, but he was the chief of the Volunteer Fire Department and he did serve as the county treasurer and as the city auditor for a while. I would assume that there must be some pictures of him in those roles."

Nelson smiled and said, "Let's see what we can find. Why don't we start by looking at the photos on the wall? They're not arranged in chronological order, but they are all labeled fairly completely."

I followed her over to the far wall and we began moving down the rows of photos. There were a lot of pictures of early pioneers—people proudly posed in front of their sod houses in their Sunday best. There were pictures of farmers out in their fields at different times of the year, and photos from the early days of Tyndall when the town was still forming up. About halfway down the wall was a smaller version of the photo hanging in the Dugout, with my grandfather leaning against the tellers' cages. And next to that was a group of pictures labeled "Fire Department, 1905."

A number of individual black and white photos had been matted and gathered into one group in a large frame. The pictures were identical, suggesting that they had all been taken at the same time. Each oval photo showed a man, dressed in his firefighters' uniform, and in the lower left-hand corner of the frame was a picture labeled "Charles Kratina."

This picture predated the photo I'd found in my mother's house by four years. My grandfather would have been twenty-seven or twenty-eight years old, depending on when the picture had been taken. He's looking directly into the camera wearing a billed cap which identifies him as a member of "Hose Co. No. 1."

His uniform jacket is buttoned to the neck, and a white shirt with a tiny bowtie peeks out over the top of the jacket. In the photo he appears to be so young, so earnest and so steadfast. He does not look remotely like a man who, twenty years down the road, would wind up betraying his family, his community, and his employer by stealing two-hundred-thousand dollars.

With Nelson's permission, I set the photo on the table and took a couple of pictures of it with my phone. She then returned the picture to the wall, and I spent a few minutes looking at several general pictures of the town taken in the 1920s. It was clearly a younger town, and many of the buildings that still lined Main Street today looked fresh and new in the photos. There was a good picture of the Security Bank from 1924, and I copied that as well.

I saw no other pictures of my grandfather and none of any of the other members of his family. None of the items exhibited on the display tables seemed to be of use with respect to my mission, and Nelson apologized for not having been more help.

"Not at all," I said. "I really appreciate the fact that you were willing to meet me here this morning. Even if I didn't find any additional material relating to my research, at least I know that I didn't leave a stone unturned. And finding that photograph was worth the trip in and of itself."

"Well, I was happy to help, even if I wasn't much help."

As we walked back toward the door, I asked her if she knew of any local descendants of sheriffs Howard and Checka. "I have an appointment this morning with Millie Hopworth who is Checka's granddaughter, but no one's been able to point me in the direction of anyone who might have been related to Howard."

"I'm afraid I'm not going to be of much help either. I know Millie, of course, but I don't think there are any Howards left in town."

"What I was really hoping to find is any records the two sheriffs might have kept from back in the Twenties. Apparently, rather than leaving their files with the office, they took them with them as their own personal property. I gather that no one has ever donated any such files to the museum?"

"I'm afraid not. I suppose it's possible that if the files survived, someone might have donated them to the State Historical Society in Pierre. You might want to check with them."

"That's a good idea. I read in the papers from that era that Sheriff Howard was killed in a hunting accident in early 1926. At least in the newspapers, the investigation seemed to peter out without ever discovering what had happened or who might have fired the shot. As a local historian, do you know anything about the case and if it was ever resolved?"

Nelson shook her head. "I do vaguely remember reading about the accident, but as far as I know, nothing ever came of the investigation. It's one of Tyndall's great unsolved mysteries."

29.

I thanked Nelson for her help, then got into the Chrysler and drove over to Mrs. Hopworth's home, which turned out to be a small white house just a block or so east of Main Street. I rang the bell promptly at eleven, and the door was opened by a heavy-set woman with steel-gray hair, parted on the right, and styled in a way that might have been in vogue maybe twenty years earlier. I introduced myself and thanked her for agreeing to see me.

She led me into a small living room that smelled vaguely of lilac. The room was jammed with furniture and knick-knacks, and, like its owner, also looked like it hadn't changed much in the last couple of decades. She invited me to sit on the couch and asked if I'd like some coffee. "Coffee would be great, if it's no trouble."

"No trouble at all," she said. "It's already made."

Hopworth left the room for a minute or so and then returned carrying a silver tray with two very delicate china cups and saucers in a pattern that almost matched the print dress she was wearing. A matching pot, a sugar bowl, and a small cream pitcher completed the collection. She set the tray on the coffee table in front of the couch and sat in a chair opposite me. Her right hand trembled a bit as she lifted the pot, but she steadied her right arm with her left hand and carefully poured the coffee without spilling a drop. She set the pot back on the tray and said, "Help yourself to cream or sugar."

"Thank you, but black is fine for me."

She nodded and poured a little cream into her own coffee. She carefully stirred the mixture, set the spoon on her saucer and then balanced the cup and saucer on her lap. Before taking a sip, she said, "You wanted to talk to me about my grandfather?"

"Yes. I understand he was the sheriff here in the late 1920s. I'm doing some research into my family who lived here at the same time."

"Did my grandfather have to arrest someone in your family?"

Smiling, I said, "No, at least I don't think so. But my grandfather took his own life just before your grandfather became the sheriff. I assume that the sheriff's office would have conducted at least a brief investigation of the incident, and I was hoping that there might still be some record of the investigation. The current sheriff—Sheriff Davis—tells me that back then, the sheriffs took their records with them when they left office. I was just wondering if, by any chance, your grandfather's records would still exist somewhere. Do you have any idea what he might have done with them?"

Hopworth finally took a sip of her coffee and then set the cup and saucer on the table between us. "Well, I don't remember ever seeing them, but if they still exist, there probably down in the basement somewhere."

I'd really expected her to tell me that if any such records had existed, they were either long gone by now or that she had no idea where they might be, and so I was more than a little surprised to hear that they might still be available after all. I set my cup and saucer on the table and said, "Do you really think there's a chance that they might still be there, Mrs. Hopworth?"

She shrugged. "I come from a family of pack rats, Mr. Oliva. This house originally belonged to my grandfather, and there are still boxes of papers and other such things down there that go all the way back to his day. If you'd like, we could go down and take a look."

"I'd certainly appreciate it, if it wouldn't be too much trouble, Ma'am."

We stood and she led me through the living room and into the kitchen. Hopworth stepped through the room and opened a door next to the Philco refrigerator. She leaned in and snapped a light on, then turned to me and said, "Why don't you go on ahead—but be careful; these stairs are a little steep."

She stepped back and allowed me to walk in front of her. The staircase was, in fact, pretty steep and led down into an unfinished basement that was nearly filled with boxes and various other items that appeared to have been stacked up somewhat haphazardly over a good many years.

Hopworth followed me down the stairs and then stopped a couple of steps short of the basement floor. "I need to keep this dress clean for my doctor's appointment, and so I'll let you take a look and see if the papers you're looking for might be here. Pointing at a set of shelves filled with cardboard file boxes, she said, "Granddad's stuff is at the end of the shelves near the far wall."

I made my way over to the shelves and stepped over to the boxes she had indicated. I saw several with labels indicating that they contained correspondence, records relating to taxes and other such matters. By the years indicated on the labels, these boxes were too recent to be records left by Hopworth's grandfather. I spent a few minutes carefully scanning the labels and then, on the bottom row, I spied two boxes, one labeled "Sheriff Checka, 1925-1934," and another labeled "Sheriff Checka, 1935-1940."

I pulled the first box from the shelf and set it on the floor. The lid was covered with dust and looking at it, I concluded that it had been a very long time since anyone had checked its contents. I removed the lid and carefully set it aside. Jammed into the box were manila file folders that apparently contained a variety of documents related to the earlier years of Checka's term. After quickly examining the labels on some of the files, I put the lid back on the box, then used my handkerchief to wipe off the dust. I then set the second box on top of the first and wiped the dust off that as well.

Refolding the handkerchief so as to contain the dust, I picked up the two boxes and carried them over to the steps where Hopworth was waiting. I set the boxes on the floor in front of her and said, "This looks like the material I was hoping to find. I'd certainly appreciate an opportunity to go through it."

She looked at the two boxes and said, "Well, Mr. Oliva, as far as I'm concerned, you're welcome to have them."

Somewhat surprised, I looked up at her and said, "Are you sure, Ma'am? I'd be happy to go through the boxes and then return them to you."

"No, really, that's quite all right. I don't know what I'd ever do with them and I've been thinking for a while now that it's time I started getting rid of all this junk. I'm not as young as I used to be and when the time comes for me to go out to Prairie View or wherever, I don't want to leave this huge mess for my children to have to deal with."

It occurred to me that, if anything, Hopworth was at least a few years younger than I was. Clearly, though, she had either surrendered to the idea that she had become an "old lady," or, as the condition of her house suggested, she had been locked in a time capsule for about the last forty years, somewhat like one of those prehistoric bugs trapped in amber. I wasn't about to argue with her, though. If she wanted to let me take the material, I'd be happy to do so. Once I was finished with it, I could then offer it either to the library or the museum.

I picked up the two boxes and followed her back up the stairs and through the house to the front door. I set the boxes on the floor next to the door and turned back to Hopworth, who was standing in the middle of the living room. "Would you like to finish your coffee, Mr. Oliva? I could reheat it."

"Thank you, Mrs. Hopworth. I appreciate the offer, but it's getting close to noon and I don't want to make you late for your doctor's appointment."

She looked down at the delicate watch on her left wrist. "Oh my, it is later than I thought, and I do need to be going."

"I'll get out of your way then, and again, I want to thank you very much for allowing me to take these papers."

"That's quite all right, Mr. Oliva. I hope they're of some use to you."

30.

Hopworth held the door for me as I picked up the boxes and walked them out to the car. I secured them in the trunk, then waved goodbye to her as she stood on the porch, watching me off. I decided that the best place to review the files would be at the small desk in my motel room, where I'd be undisturbed and away from prying eyes. I swung by the café and got a tuna salad sandwich and a large Coke to go, then I headed on back to the Welcome Inn.

I'd worn a pair of slacks and a dress shirt to meet with Nelson and Hopworth, and once back in my room, I changed into jeans, a tee shirt, and my tennis shoes. I opened the sandwich, took a couple of bites, and then pulled out the first of Sheriff Checka's files which was labeled "Howard Investigation."

The first items in the file were three black-and-white photographs of a man's body—apparently Sheriff Hal Howard—lying obviously dead in a wooded area. The pictures were taken from three different angles and two of the photos showed the body apparently as it had been discovered. In the third photo, the victim's heavy jacket had been unbuttoned and pulled open to reveal a major chest wound.

A serious amount of blood had leaked out and had been soaked up by the man's shirt. The shirt had been torn by the force of the bullet, but the wound itself remained hidden by the shirt and the blood. It appeared that the victim had only been shot once, and I couldn't even guess at the caliber of the round that would have done this much damage. It would have been a large one, though, and I assumed that if Howard had not been dead before falling to the ground, he would have been very close to it.

Behind the photos was a report from the coroner. Apparently, there had not been a formal autopsy, but the coroner reported that Howard's death had resulted from a single gunshot wound to the chest and that death had been instantaneous. The bullet had not been recovered and the coroner was unable to say anything about it, save for the fact that he could not determine the distance from which the shot might have been fired.

The rest of the file included interviews and witness statements regarding Howard's movements on the day of his death. He had told his office that he was taking a Saturday off to go deer hunting and that he was going by himself. He'd had breakfast at Mindy's Diner at six-thirty that morning, and the counterman said that he'd left about seven. The counterman was the last person Checka could find who had seen Howard alive.

At eleven fifteen that morning, another hunter named Pete Slavinsky, who was hunting with two friends, stumbled across Howard's body in a wooded area fourteen miles northeast of town. Slavinsky raced back to his truck, drove to a farmhouse a couple of miles away, and called the sheriff's office. Gary Checka and two other deputies had responded to the scene, along with a local doctor, even though Slavinsky had apparently assured Checka that it was too late for the doctor to do any good.

Reading the file, it was clear that, from the beginning, Checka and the other investigators had concluded that this was nothing more sinister than a simple hunting accident. The main thrust of the investigation had centered on efforts to discover who else might have been hunting in the area that morning and who might have accidentally fired the fatal shot. As the newspaper report had suggested, the investigators assumed that the person who fired the shot may have failed to realize that he had hit another hunter.

The acting sheriff and his deputies had tracked down eleven other hunters who had been in the general area that morning. Like Howard, some of them had been hunting alone; others in pairs. None of them remembered having seen Howard at any time that morning. Interestingly, one of the other hunters interviewed was George Benson. Benson told Checka that he'd left his home about six o'clock and had driven alone directly to the hunting grounds. He parked on land belonging to a farmer that was a friend of his and walked into the woods at around six-thirty.

Like the other hunters, he said that he had not seen Howard, although he had briefly encountered two of the other men who had been out in the woods that morning. Benson said that he had seen no deer and had not fired his rifle. He left the woods a little before ten, returned home, and changed his clothes for a meeting at the farm implement dealership at eleven.

Behind the witness statements was a sheet containing a series of questions that Checka had apparently posed to himself regarding the $8700 dollars that had been later found in Hal Howard's safe deposit box. He had circled the figure $8700 and followed it with three question marks.

He had also written "Bribes???," then crossed that out and wrote "No!" Another note said, "Financial problems???" Again, "No."

"Inheritance??? Who would have died? No."

"Savings???"

Checka appeared to be a man who clearly liked his question marks, but in the end, he was apparently unable to come up with a satisfactory answer to any of them, and at the end of the sheet was a short sentence that said, "Return the money to Doris."

Stapled to that page were interview notes from Howard's wife and from his former banker, a guy named Elmer Carlsen at the First National Bank. Both insisted that Howard was not in financial difficulty and did not owe money to anyone save for a mortgage on his home. The monthly payments were relatively small and certainly would not appear to have been a problem, as evidenced by the fact that Howard always made the payment a couple of days early and had never once been late.

Carlsen indicated that Howard kept a modest balance in his checking account at the bank and that he had no savings account, perhaps confirming his wife's statement to the effect that Howard had not trusted banks. The money in the safe deposit box had been divided by denomination and had been bundled and wrapped with rubber bands.

The collection had not included any one-dollar bills, and the rest of the bills appeared to have been in circulation for some time. None of them had been printed in sequence, all of which confirmed Mrs. Howard's suggestion that her husband had accumulated the savings over a long period of time, and which apparently led to Checka's recommendation that the money should be returned to the widow.

And that was it. Checka had not written, or at least he hadn't left in the file, any notes containing his final thoughts on the investigation. I wondered what he had thought about it all. Did he assume that the person who had fired the shot that killed Howard was actually unaware he had done so? Did he perhaps believe that the person knew or suspected that he had fired the shot but was refusing to admit it? Was he simply leaving the file open pending further developments, or had he concluded, as Anna Nelson suggested, that Howard's death would remain a mystery?

It occurred to me that I was a man with a lot of questions marks myself, but sitting at the desk in my motel room, I didn't have any more answers than Gary Checka had found over ninety years earlier.

* * *

The rest of the files in the box were labeled with the months of the year, beginning with February 1926, and contained summaries of the incidents that the sheriff's office had investigated during those particular months. The activities ran the gamut from lost children and pets to drunk driving, neighborhood disputes, marital squabbles and an occasional robbery or bar fight. The crime rate in Bon Homme county appeared to be fairly low, and quickly scanning the files, I didn't find another suspicious death until October of 1928.

A woman had been found stabbed to death in her home by her adult daughter who had come over to visit. The daughter reported that her mother and her stepfather had been at odds and that the stepfather had beaten her mother from time to time. The sheriff's office had apparently been called to intervene in the couple's disagreements on several occasions, and deputies found the victim's husband drunk in a bar in Tabor, South Dakota, a couple of miles from his home. They arrested the man who immediately confessed to the crime and allegedly told the deputies that he would never regret what he'd done for a single goddamned minute.

I found nothing in the first box that appeared to bear on any subject in which I was interested. I opened the second box to find a similar set of files running through the remainder of Checka's tenure as county sheriff. Behind those were a set of files containing the budgets for the Sheriff's Department from 1924 to 1940. The first of the files, containing the budgets for 1924-1925, was labeled in a hand different than Checka's. I assumed that Howard, the previous sheriff, had probably labeled the file and that, since it contained the budget for the year in which he had taken over the office, Checka had simply kept it with his own files when he inherited the job.

Behind the file containing the department's budget for 1940, were several other file folders that had been bound together by a length of twine. Again, the file labels had clearly been printed by a hand different than Checka's, and curious, I pulled them out of the box. Slipped under the string that bound the files together was a piece of notepaper that said, "Howard."

I cut the string, freeing the files, and opened the first one to discover that I was looking at files that had been created by Checka's predecessor. I had no idea if I was looking at the complete set of files from his seven-year term, but if the first file folder was representative, Howard had not kept records nearly as complete even as the relatively thin records kept by his successor.

The file was labeled "1918-1920," and contained only a few summary notes regarding the activity of the Sheriff's Department during that period. Unable to contain my curiosity, I went immediately to the file dated "1924-1925." Like the first file, the entries were sparse, and I couldn't begin to believe that they reflected all of the activities, even of a department this tiny in a county with a population this small.

I quickly flipped through the pages related to actions that the department had taken in 1924 and early 1925. I then came to a page dated May 20, 1925 on which Howard had written, "Called to Security Bank at 8:30 a.m. Discovered that Charlie Kratina had killed himself with a shotgun in the vault. Body discovered by teller Alan Morris when he came to open the bank for business. Coroner arrived and pronounced the victim dead as a suicide. Removed body to funeral home.

"Took possession of suicide note and sent Dale to notify Charlie's wife. Morris says C.G. and George Benson in Sioux Falls, due back this aft. Called C.G. at hotel in S.F. Told Morris to close the bank for the day and agreed it would be all right to have someone come in and begin cleaning up so the bank could open for business tomorrow."

The next notes, apparently written later in the day, said, "2:30 p.m. Talked with C. G. and Benson. Showed them Charlie's note and asked what he might have been sorry for. C.G. says examiners discovered shortages in bank accounts. Charlie suspected of embezzlement. C.G. and Benson called to S.F. to talk with regulators. Charlie must have known thefts about to be discovered and so killed himself rather than go to prison. C.G. insists bank will be fine. Wants to keep shortages quiet for the moment, until he can issue a public statement. Agreed to say that we have no idea why Charlie might have killed himself."

And that was, apparently, the extent of Sheriff Howard's "investigation" into my grandfather's death. In fairness, though, things seemed pretty straightforward, especially since my grandfather had been courteous enough to leave a note.

I remembered that C. G. Webster was the bank's president. Certainly, he would have worried that a run on the bank might have occurred had news of the shortages leaked out. I wondered if he believed that the bank could still be saved or if he already knew that it was doomed and was simply looking for time enough to plan an orderly reorganization. I also couldn't help but wonder if he and the bank's board members had withdrawn their own money from the bank while there was still time to do so.

I wondered if Sheriff Howard had actually bought Webster's argument that the bank would be fine, or if he suspected that it might be in danger. Whichever the case, he apparently went along with the program and made no public mention of the reason why my grandfather might have taken his own life. My grandfather had died on a Wednesday morning, and the bank had been closed for the day. It was apparently open for business again on Thursday morning, and my grandfather was buried on Friday. Case closed.

I set the page aside, determined to keep it for myself, and then went through the remaining files that Howard had left, which made no further mention of my grandfather or of the problems at the bank. The third-to-the-last file was marked "Jensen," and included notes on a murder-suicide, or perhaps, really, a double suicide, involving an elderly farmer and his wife. Their farm was failing and apparently the bank was about to foreclose and evict them. Before that could happen, the couple arranged their affairs and then laid down together on their bed where the husband apparently shot his wife and then himself.

The second-to-last folder was fairly thick and labeled "Budgets, 1918-1921." It included copies of the budgets that the county had apparently allotted for the department during those years. The last folder was labeled "Budgets, 1921-1923." This seemed to confirm my assumption that when he assumed the office, Checka had kept Howard's budget files for 1924-1925 for his own use and had bound Howard's previous budget files with the remainder of his files.

I flipped open the folder to find budget sheets similar to those I'd seen in the earlier files. But at the back of the folder was a sealed tan envelope, ten by thirteen inches. It had been folded in half and was effectively concealed by the documents in front of it, all of which were on standard sheets of paper, eight and a half by eleven.

I unfolded the envelope and turned it over in my hands. It had faded a bit over time and was not labeled in any way. I wondered how long it might have been sitting in the file folder and who might have put it there. Curious, I got out my small pocketknife, opened the blade and slit the top of the envelope. I returned the knife to my pocket, pulled out the contents of the envelope, and found myself looking at a black-and-white photograph of my grandfather, lying dead on the floor in the vault of the Security Bank of Tyndall.

31.

The picture had been taken from just outside the door leading into the vault. My grandfather had apparently been sitting on a stool, facing the door, with the shotgun balanced on a stack of books that had been piled on the floor to his right. The force of the blast had knocked him off the stool, which had then tipped over and fallen next to him. The body was lying on a diagonal line across the middle of the room, and the damage was extensive. Clearly, he had died instantly.

Two other photos showed the body from different angles but didn't appear to add any additional information. My grandfather had died wearing a dark suit along with a white shirt and tie. His shoes looked freshly shined, and I wondered if he might have been determined to die, dressed for the occasion. The shotgun was lying on the floor to the right of his body. Looking closely, I didn't see his suicide note anywhere in the vault, and I wondered where it might have been found.

Behind the pictures was a report apparently written after Howard had interviewed my grandmother. According to his notes, my grandmother said that my grandfather had eaten a slice of toast with a cup of coffee before leaving for work a little after seven o'clock, which was at least an hour earlier than usual. He had explained that he had an early appointment at the bank and said that he would be home at the usual time for dinner. On the way out the door, he hugged his five-year-old daughter, Marie, and promised his twelve-year-old son, Chuck, that he would help him with his math homework that evening.

My grandmother insisted that his attitude on leaving home that morning had been perfectly normal. In recent days and weeks, my grandfather had not appeared worried or stressed, and he had been sleeping normally. He'd not suggested that there were any problems at work, and he'd given no hint at all that he might be thinking of taking his own life.

My grandmother also told the sheriff that the family was not in any financial difficulty and that, at least as far as she knew, my grandfather had not come into any newfound wealth. She allowed that my grandfather had been talking about buying a "new" used car, and they had been trying to decide if the price of the car would fit into their budget.

A check with the bank indicated that my grandfather had a small balance in his checking account and a little over a thousand dollars in his savings account. He and my grandmother were carrying a modest mortgage on their home but appeared to have no other outstanding debts.

In his notes, Howard wrote that my grandmother had been clearly devastated by the news and that she had refused to believe that her husband might have taken his own life, even when shown his suicide note. She seemed not to know how her family might survive in the absence of her husband.

When questioned, neither Webster, the bank president, nor George Benson, the head cashier, had any explanation for why my grandfather would have been going into work early. According to Benson, he and my grandfather usually both arrived at the bank at eight-thirty, half an hour before the bank opened for business.

Alan Morris, the teller who had discovered the body, had no explanation either. Morris told the sheriff that he had arrived at work a little before eight thirty and had let himself in through the side door, which was the entrance that employees normally used. The bank was quiet; the lights were off, and Morris assumed that he was the first employee to get in that morning. He snapped on the lights, walked straight to his desk, removed his suit coat, and set it over the back of his chair. Only then did he turn and realize that the door to the vault was standing open.

Morris said that he walked over to the door of the vault and saw my grandfather's body lying there. On seeing the body, he ran immediately to the restroom where he threw up into the toilet. He then cleaned himself up and called the sheriff's office without returning to the vault. While waiting for the sheriff to arrive, Morris found the suicide note lying on my grandfather's desk.

Based on the way the blood had pooled around my grandfather's body, the coroner estimated that he had been dead for a little over an hour before Morris discovered him. During the course of my career, I'd seen enough shooting victims to understand that this could be little more than a wild guess, but in fairness, the science in these matters was not nearly as sophisticated in 1925 as it was more than ninety years later. Howard's deputies interviewed other people who were normally in that area of town between seven and eight o'clock on a weekday morning, but none of them reported hearing the shot.

That surprised me a bit. A shotgun blast would have made a helluva lot of noise, even allowing for the bank's brick walls which would have muffled the sound a bit. Even at that hour of the morning, and especially in a farming community, it seemed impossible to imagine that no one would have heard it.

In separate interviews, Webster and Benson told the sheriff that bank examiners had discovered the shortages in the bank's accounts the previous week and that the two of them had been called to meet with bank regulators in Sioux Falls to discuss the matter. That, along with my grandfather's note, appeared to provide an explanation for why he had committed suicide, but both Webster and Benson claimed that they had no idea where the missing money might have gone.

The two told Howard that my grandfather had been out of town only briefly during the course of the past year and had been no farther away than Sioux Falls. The only logical explanation, then, was that he had been working with a confederate. In his interview, Webster suggested that the confederate must have held on to the money and that my grandfather had not been given his share yet. When the sheriff asked the president how that much money could have gone missing from the bank without anyone at the bank noticing it, Webster told Howard that he would "have to talk to George about that."

The sheriff apparently *did* raise the issue with Benson, and it seemed a logical question: how could the bank's assistant cashier steal that much money without the head cashier being aware of it?

As the newspaper accounts had indicated, Benson had initially insisted that he *was* unaware of the thefts, and his original explanation to Howard rested on the way my grandfather had carried out the scheme. When the bad checks his confederate or confederates had written were returned to the bank, my grandfather had hidden or destroyed them, making no notation of the bank's losses in the books. As for the missing certificates of deposit, Benson pointed out that they had been removed from books of CDs that the bank would not normally have gotten to for quite some time, and insisted that neither he nor anyone else had had occasion to check those books until the auditors arrived.

The explanation had apparently sounded as lame to the sheriff as it had to the bank's Board, and, as the newspapers had reported, within a couple of days, Benson changed his tune. He then admitted that he had discovered that money was missing due to the bad checks and had opted to allow my grandfather the opportunity to repay the money rather than reporting him.

The notes that Howard had included in this file were more detailed than the ones he had included on the single page I'd found in the file for 1924-1925, but they raised more questions than answers, and I found myself wishing that he had made more complete notes of his interviews, particularly with Benson and

Webster, and that he had taken at least a little time to summarize his own thoughts about the investigation.

I flipped to the next page and found a sheet of random notes and doodles that I assumed had been made by the sheriff while he was perhaps thinking through the situation. At the top of the page, he had written, "C.K.-L.H.", and had circled the initials. C.K. was clearly my grandfather, but who was "L.H."? In my research, I hadn't encountered anyone with those initials. Was the sheriff speculating about someone who might possibly have been my grandfather's accomplice in the scheme?

He'd also written the word, "Noise?" perhaps wondering as I did how it was possible that no one outside the bank had heard the shotgun blast. Next to that, were the words, "Door closed?"

Howard knew that the exterior doors to the bank were closed and locked when my grandfather fired the shot. Could he have been referring to the door to the vault? I assumed that, had my grandfather closed the door to the vault before firing the shot, the thickness of the walls of the steel vault would have been enough to contain the sound of the blast.

Returning to the photos, I looked at the vault door which was standing wide open out into the room. Was this how the teller had found it, or had the door been only partially open when he got there? I assumed that if the door had not already been wide open when they arrived, the sheriff and his team would have moved the door to that position. If my grandfather had closed the door without securing it before he fired the shot, could the door have then swung open a bit on its own before Morris arrived? At this late date, there was simply no way of knowing. It appeared, though, that Sheriff Howard had been thinking along these lines. I wondered if he had experimented with the door, and if so, what he might have found.

On the page, Howard had made a number of random doodles and had also written, "Benson/Daniels?" That was followed by the figures, "$200,000 ($20,000)?" I assumed that the two hundred-thousand-dollar figure referred to the amount of money missing from the bank. I had no idea what the Twenty-thousand-dollar reference might mean or why the figures were tied to the two names.

In the middle of the page, Howard had written the name "Calvin Webb," followed by a question mark. I had no idea who Calvin Webb might be until I flipped to the next page and found a signed witness statement that Howard had taken from Webb on May 21, 1925. In the statement, Webb said that he had been making his normal rounds for the Tyndall Dairy at 6:50 a.m. on Wednesday, May 20, when he saw Joseph Daniels letting himself into the Security Bank through the side door. Webb said that he saw no one else in the immediate vicinity and that he did not believe that Daniels had noticed him driving by in his dairy truck.

Who was Joseph Daniels?

I remembered that Bud Daniels had told me that his grandfather had served on the bank's Board of Directors. Could this be him, and if so, what in the hell was he doing in the Security Bank only minutes before my grandfather arrived and shot himself? And why was there no mention of this interview anywhere else in the files? Armed with this information, Howard certainly must have interviewed Daniels, but where were the notes from that interview?

There was nothing else in the file, and I couldn't help but wonder if part of it was missing or if some of the material might have been destroyed for some reason. I'd earlier concluded that Howard's record-keeping left a lot to be desired and now I found the lack of information in his files to be thoroughly frustrating. In particular, who was "L.H.," and what was his—or her—connection to my grandfather? Why had Howard made the reference, and who might he have been thinking of?

I sat back in the chair, shaking my head and wondering what Hal Howard might have concluded about all of this. Unfortunately, though, his spirit opted not to reach down through the decades and gift me with any inspiration.

* * *

I'd spent the bulk of the afternoon with the files, and by then it was four thirty. I decided that maybe the best idea was to clear my head a bit and hope that inspiration would strike me later. I was due out at my cousin's in an hour and a half, and so I made a few notes on my computer and copied the files to my flash drive. I dropped the flash drive into my pocket, locked my computer in the trunk with the files I had gotten from Mrs. Hopworth, and headed on over to the Dugout to say goodbye to Matt and to have one more beer in my grandfather's honor in the building where he had died.

32.

Tyndall, South Dakota was apparently gearing up for the weekend, and at five o'clock on a Friday evening, the Dugout was nearly full. Happy Hour was well under way, and when I made my way through the crowd and finally got to the bar, I was lucky to get the last open stool. Matt and another bartender were working at full speed to keep the drinks flowing, but he took a moment to say hello as he popped the cap off a bottle of MGD and set it in front of me. "Busy night," I said.

"Oh yeah. Tonight, I'll be workin' harder than a one-legged man in an ass-kicking contest."

It was an old joke, but I laughed anyway. Matt moved down the bar to pour a couple of drinks and I drained about half of my beer in one pull. After working all afternoon in the sheriff's dusty old files, it really hit the spot. I sat there, watching the crowd for a few minutes, then got up off the stool and wandered over to the wall for one last look at the pictures of my grandfather that were hanging there.

Standing in front of the pictures, I saluted him with the beer and thought, *well, Grandpa, I came here looking for answers and instead, it looks like I'm going to be leaving with more questions than I had when I got here.*

My grandfather made no response and instead simply stood in front of the teller's cages staring at me from the one photo, while he continued to sit at his desk and sign his papers in the other. I'd been looking at the pictures for a couple of minutes or so, when out of nowhere, the tumblers in my mind turned one more time and the pins suddenly dropped into place.

I stood there for another minute, looking at the photos and slowly shaking my head. Then I reached out and touched a finger to my grandfather's face before making my way back to the bar. I waved Matt over and asked him how late he'd be open. "Midnight on Fridays, or later if we've still got a decent crowd."

"Great." I dug the flash drive out of my pocket and slid it across the bar. "Hang onto this for me, will you? I'll pick it up later tonight. If for some reason, I don't get back, give it to Sheriff Davis tomorrow, okay?"

Matt appeared to take the request in stride and said, "No problem, Jack. I'll look for you later tonight."

I thanked him, dropped a twenty on the bar, and wove my way back through the crowd and out to my Chrysler. Then I headed north out of town for dinner with my cousin, Bud.

Four miles out of town, and three miles south of Bud's place, I turned right onto a gravel road that paralleled the soybean field from which someone had taken a shot at me on Wednesday night. The road ran straight as an arrow to the east and I assumed it had been laid out along a section line. I followed the road for a mile until it met another gravel road that ran due north and south. I sat at the intersection of the two roads for a couple of minutes, calculating time and distance, then headed back west toward the highway and from there turned north to my cousin's farm.

33.

When I pulled to a stop in front of the house, I found Bud sitting on the porch with a beer in his hand and Cody lying by his side. Bud gave a wave and stood as I got out of the car. Coming down to greet me, he slapped me on the back and said, "Good to see you, Jack. Take a load off and let me grab you a beer."

I followed him onto the porch and dropped into the chair next to his. He pulled a Stella from a Styrofoam cooler next to his chair, popped the top and handed it to me. Tapping his bottle to mine, he said, "Here's to the weekend."

"I'll drink to that," I said.

Although still a bit warm, it was another very nice evening. Across the lawn, a field of corn blew gently in the light breeze and high in the clear blue sky, a hawk circled, looking for some unsuspecting prey. Bud took a pull on his beer and said, "So, back to the big city tomorrow, huh?"

"Yup; it's time. Tyndall seems like a nice little town, but I miss the rhythm of Phoenix, and I'm missing my girlfriend as well."

He nodded. "So, how did your research turn out? Did you find what you were looking for?"

I waited a couple of beats and then said, "Yeah, I did. Some things I'll never know for sure, let alone ever be able to prove, but I've now got a pretty clear idea of what actually happened up here all those years ago."

He looked over as if appraising me, then said, "And what did you learn?"

I sat there for a moment, playing with the label on my beer bottle, then turned to face him. "Your grandfather didn't make a killing in the stock market, did he, Bud?"

"What the hell makes you say a thing like that?"

"Perhaps I should rephrase it. Maybe he did make a killing in the market. But if he did, I assume that the seed money came out of the funds that he and George Benson stole from the Security Bank."

Bud stood and walked across the porch. Then he turned to face me again, leaning back against the porch railing. "You're out of your goddamned mind, Cousin."

"No, I'm not, *Cousin*, and you damn well know it. Your grandfather, almost certainly acting together with George Benson, was embezzling money from the bank. When the bank examiners began to suspect the fraud, your grandfather and Benson needed a fall guy. They nominated my grandfather for the role and early one morning while Benson was safely in Sioux Falls with a perfect alibi, your grandfather lured mine to the bank on some pretext or other, walked him into the vault, and shot him to death.

"Your grandfather also scrawled an approximation of my grandfather's signature on a note he'd typed up in which my grandfather appeared to confess to stealing the money from the bank and he placed the note on my grandfather's desk. He then slipped out of the bank, leaving a teller who arrived an hour later to discover my grandfather's 'suicide.'"

Bud smiled. "You are totally fuckin' nuts."

He sat back down in his chair, pulled two more beers from the cooler and popped the tops. He set one on the table next to me, took a pull from his own, and said, "Go on, Cuz. This is totally off the rails, but it's very entertaining. So, what happened next?"

"What happened next was that the sheriff arrived on the scene and initially accepted the idea that my grandfather had taken his own life. Benson and the bank's president raced home from Sioux Falls and told the sheriff that there were shortages in the bank's funds. Benson initially claimed that he knew nothing about the shortages, which of course was pure bullshit. He was the bank's head cashier. There's no way in hell that the bank would be short nearly two hundred thousand dollars without him knowing about it.

"Then, a couple of days later, Benson 'confessed' that he really had known that at least some of the money was missing. He said that my grandfather had admitted stealing it and that he had promised to return it. Benson said that he agreed to give him some time to do so, but then the bank examiners showed up and discovered the money was missing. Benson and the bank president told the sheriff that my grandfather had probably killed himself because he didn't want to be exposed and wind up in jail."

I took a pull on the second beer and continued. "At any rate, that became the official story. The money was gone. My grandfather took it. He killed himself. And his accomplice got away with the money, which was never recovered. Everything was all wrapped up in a nice, neat package.

"But, of course, my grandfather really didn't kill himself. He didn't take the money, and the money wasn't really missing. Your grandfather and Benson had it, and they were very, very careful with it. Rather than starting to spend the money extravagantly, which might well have raised suspicions, they held onto it. Shit, Bud, maybe your grandfather really *did* park his share in the market for a couple of years.

"Whatever the case, three years down the road, Benson and your grandfather both enjoyed a bit of good fortune. Your grandfather made a killing in the market, allowing him to begin buying up land from farmers who were in distress, and Benson's dear old long-lost uncle died, leaving him money enough to buy the farm implement dealership. Meanwhile, my poor grandmother was taking in laundry and sending two of her sons off to live with relatives because she couldn't afford to keep them at home"

"Well, Jack, it's a very interesting story, and I don't know how in the hell you ever came up with it, but you can't have an ounce of proof to support it."

"Actually, I do. It turns out that the sheriff might not have been as dumb as he pretended to be. The suicide scene that your grandfather arranged, didn't look quite right to the sheriff and he began poking into it. He turned up a witness—a milkman—who saw your grandfather letting himself into the bank about thirty minutes before my grandfather was murdered."

"So what? Even if my grandfather *had* gone into the bank, that doesn't mean that he was still there when your grandfather shot himself, and it sure as hell doesn't mean that my grandfather killed him."

"Yeah, it does. Your grandfather fucked up, and the sheriff caught him at it. First of all, nobody outside the bank heard the noise of the shotgun blast. You know damned good and well that someone would have, unless maybe the door to the vault was closed when the shot was fired.

"I wondered about that, and the sheriff did too. The door to the vault was standing open when the teller arrived and found my grandfather's body, and my grandfather sure as hell hadn't opened it after shooting himself. If your grandfather would have had sense enough to close the vault door again after he left, that might not have aroused suspicion."

"There's a whole lot of supposition hanging off a very thin thread there, Cousin."

"Yeah, well, that wasn't your grandfather's worst mistake. He set the stage wrong, Bud. My grandfather was sitting on a stool in the vault when your grandfather shot him. Either before or after killing him, your grandfather stacked some books to the right of the stool, as if the shotgun had been resting on the books. My grandfather was shot from the right side and fell to his left. The shotgun was lying on the right side of his body."

I took a sip of the beer and looked over at my cousin. "My grandfather was left-handed, Bud. I didn't realize it until late this afternoon when I looked again at a picture of him signing some documents. And the thing is, the sheriff saw the same thing, and he made a note. He wrote the initials, 'C.K.-L.H.' and circled them. When I saw the note in his files, I thought that the letters 'L.H.' were someone's initials, maybe someone the sheriff suspected of being my grandfather's accomplice. But they weren't. The sheriff knew that my grandfather was lefthanded and that the whole scene was wrong."

"Well, dammit, Jack, *if* the sheriff was so fuckin' brilliant, and *if* he had this great witness, why didn't he arrest my grandfather and charge him with murder?"

"Because instead, he apparently decided to cut himself in on the action. In his notes he wrote the figure $200,000, followed by the figure $20,000. This part actually *is* supposition, and I can't really prove it, but the circumstantial evidence is fairly strong. I think the sheriff approached your grandfather and/or George Benson and told them that he had them by the short hairs. I'm guessing he demanded ten percent of the money they'd stolen. Maybe he settled for half of that or maybe they gave him a down payment, but shortly after that the sheriff was murdered, and when they opened his safe deposit box at the bank, they found $8700.00 that nobody could account for."

Bud shook his head. "The poor fuckin' sheriff was murdered too? Jesus, Jack."

"Well, as I said, I can't prove this part, but a few months after my grandfather was murdered the sheriff died in what appeared to be a hunting accident. They never figured out who fired the fatal shot, but that very conveniently ended any threat that the sheriff might have posed to Benson or your grandfather. And curiously, one of the other men hunting out in the same general area the morning the sheriff was shot, was George Benson. Maybe they figured that since your grandfather had done the dirty work killing my grandfather, it was Benson's turn when it came time to eliminate the sheriff."

"And you discovered all this how, Jack?"

"The sheriff kept notes of his investigation and of his suppositions, but he didn't put them in his regular files. He sealed them up in an unmarked envelope and put them in a file with the department's budgets. When he was killed, the acting sheriff bundled up his files and put them into storage, apparently without seeing the envelope. It was still sealed when I found it this afternoon and opened it."

"Well Jesus, Jack, I hope you put all that evidence in a very safe place."

"Not to worry, Bud, I did."

Bud opened another beer and offered it to me, but I said, "Not for me, thanks."

He took a long swallow from the bottle and then turned back to me. "So, what in the hell makes you think that I'd know anything about all of this?"

"Because, you dumb son of a bitch, you took a shot at me when I left here the other night. Some damned cousin you turned out to be."

"*I* took a shot at you?"

"Yeah, you did. You stood here on this very porch, waving goodbye to me all friendly-like, and the second I turned down the road, you jumped into your truck or whatever and raced across that field over there to the gravel road that runs south from here. You got to the intersection with the road running east and west, raced west down the road and set up in that soybean field.

"In the meantime, I was poking along like a goddamned ninety-eight-year-old tourist out there in the dark, and when you saw me go by, you fired off a shot. Tell me, Bud, were you really trying to hit me or just scare me off?"

He took another long pull on the beer and then smiled. "Whichever. Actually, you seemed like a nice guy, and I really didn't want to kill you, but I did want you to get the hell out of town and leave all this business alone. As soon as you left, I told Becky I had to quickly run out and check on an irrigation valve. I jumped on an ATV with a rifle I keep in the barn and raced down there, just like you figured."

"But why would you have ever thought that I posed any sort of a threat to you?"

"Because you're right. Even though people, especially in my family, believed it for years, I knew that story about my grandfather making money in the stock market was a lot of bullshit. My gramma kept a diary, Jack. I bet my grandad didn't even know it. He died before she did and my dad gave the thing to me, thinking I might be interested in it.

"She wrote a lot about being a girl out here and what life was like. She wrote about marrying my grandfather and about how they began their life together. I don't know if my dad ever started reading the thing, but he wasn't much of a reader, and he certainly wasn't much for history, and so if he did, I'm sure he got bored and stopped reading before he was halfway through it.

"I didn't stop. I read it all the way to the end, and believe me, Jack, her entries for the middle 1920s were very interesting. It turns out that my grandfather made most of the same stupid mistakes that a lot of other farmers made during and after World War I, and that he was in at least as much trouble as the rest of them when the farm economy collapsed in the Twenties.

"My gramma wrote about the hard times and about the mounting debts and about low farm prices. Late in 1924, my grandfather tried to borrow money from the Security Bank, and they turned him down. I wonder, Jack, was it your grandfather—his own brother-in-law—who told him no?

"My gramma wrote about your grandfather's death, and like everyone else around here, she bought the story that he had embezzled money from the bank and then killed himself. She couldn't believe that he would do something like that, and she was heartbroken, especially for your grandmother and her family.

"And then things on my grandparents' farm suddenly started getting better, and my gramma couldn't figure out how it had happened. But all of a sudden there was money enough to hold off the bank for at least a while. My grandfather told her that he had borrowed it from a bank in Sioux Falls, but she couldn't figure out how. If the bank here in Tyndall wouldn't loan him money, why would some bank in Sioux Falls give it to him?

"But of course, those were the days when the man was the head of the household and the 'Little Woman' didn't dare question his authority or his actions. And you can be damn sure that was the case with my grandad. My gramma might have given voice to her doubts and concerns in her secret diary, but she wouldn't have ever dared to raise them with her husband.

"I don't know if she ever suspected that my grandfather might have killed yours—I'm sure she couldn't have imagined a thing like that—but she did worry about how my grandfather had been able to turn the ship around. She knew that something wasn't right.

"After reading the diary, I realized that the damned thing could be a problem if it fell into the wrong hands and so as soon as I finished reading it, I burned it. Then, twenty-five years down the road, you showed up—a former homicide detective looking into your grandfather's death.

"I didn't know for sure, and I still don't know for sure, if my grandfather could have been involved in that business at the bank, and I couldn't imagine that even if he was, you could ever find any proof of it. But you made me nervous, Jack, and so, on an impulse, after having a couple of beers and half a bottle of wine, I decided to try to scare you off. Stupid, I know, but there you have it."

He drained the last of the beer and set the bottle next to the four others he had lined up on the table between us. "So, what do you intend to do about all of this, Cousin?"

"First, tell me one other thing, Bud. Did you leave the note at the library warning me off the other day?"

My cousin smiled and gave a small nod in my direction. "Yeah. When Meg introduced us in the café on Tuesday, it occurred to me that if you started digging into this business deeply enough it might potentially cause problems for me. To be honest, I really didn't think there was much of a chance that would happen, and I really didn't think that sending you the note was likely to scare you off, but I figured I had nothing to lose by trying. I typed it up on my computer Tuesday night and then stuck it in the door at the library early Wednesday morning. Obviously, a waste of my time."

"Obviously. And did you send that asshole Alex Benson after me?"

"Yeah. I thought that might muddy the waters a bit and throw you off stride."

"Does he know how his great grandfather was able to buy the dealership?"

"Oh, hell no. For all his pretensions, that boy is at least several bricks shy of a full load, and gullible as hell. I'm one of his better customers and Thursday morning, I called him and told him that you were investigating the death of your grandfather and that you'd told me that you thought that his great-grandfather was probably the real thief.

"Poor Alex got up on his high horse, going on about protecting his family's good name and insisting that he wasn't going to let you get away with any crap like that. I gather that he confronted you in the library, but I guess he didn't scare you any more than my note did."

"Not hardly, Bud. But while we're on the subject, did you also break into my motel room?"

He seemed genuinely surprised by the question. "No, this is the first I've heard of that. Maybe Alex showed some initiative, trying to see what sort of dirt you might have had on his precious great-grandfather."

"But you did attack Benson last night and plant the damned weapon in my car."

Again, he smiled. "Yeah, after Alex challenged you at the library, he called and told me that you'd denied claiming that his great-grandfather was involved in the thefts from the bank. I told him that of course you'd deny it but that you really did say it. That got him pissed off all over again.

"I knew, of course, that he'd be playing cards last night. Alex seems to sincerely believe that he's the greatest poker player since Doc Holliday, and he's always bragging about how well he does in that stupid game over in Yankton. So many people know about it that it's actually pretty surprising that no one's ever tried to waylay him on his way home and steal his winnings—assuming that there actually are any and that Alex isn't completely full of shit about that too.

"At any rate, having convinced Becky that this would be a good weekend for her to go up and visit her mom, I drove into town last night and parked a couple of blocks away from Benson's house. Then I jammed up the mechanism on his gate and hid behind a tree across the street, waiting for him to get home.

"I'd been waiting there for about thirty minutes when he finally showed up and stopped in front of the gate. When it wouldn't open, he got out, sort of stumbling like he was a little drunk, and went over to see what was wrong. I slipped up behind him, smacked him in the head, and went through his pockets. I took

207

his wallet and his watch and, I'm sorry to say, the stupid bastard only had thirty-seven bucks in his pocket—some big winner he was.

"Anyhow, I raced back to my car, drove over and parked a block away from the Welcome Inn. I came up from behind the motel, pulled the plastic away from your back window, and put the bat on the back seat. Then I taped up the window again, went back to my car and drove home. I was hoping that the sheriff would put two and two together and maybe throw you in the can for assault, distracting your attention away from your research project. Naturally, I also hoped that once you managed to get out from under it all, you'd get the hell out of Tyndall as fast as you could and forget all about this business. I have to say, I was sincerely disappointed when the sheriff didn't arrest you and get you out of my hair."

"Well, fortunately for me, he's a reasonably bright guy. He saw through your scheme from the git go, even though he didn't know who might have been trying to set me up."

My cousin nodded his head at that and then looked in the direction of the cooler, apparently trying to decide if he wanted another beer. Then he looked over to me and said, "So again, Jack, what are you going to do now?"

"Well, I won't be going home tomorrow. I intend to be at the sheriff's office bright and early. I'll ask him to open a new investigation into my grandfather's death and into the theft of the money from the bank. After ninety years, my grandfather deserves a chance to finally have his name cleared."

"At the expense of ruining my grandfather's reputation, and mine as well?"

"What can I say, Bud? Your damned grandfather shouldn't have killed mine and then let him take the blame for the money that your grandfather and Benson stole from the bank. But, really, why in the hell should this bother you? You said the other night that I wasn't responsible for the crime my grandfather allegedly committed. Well, *you* aren't guilty of the crime your grandfather committed either. And you still haven't told me why you feel so strongly about this that you'd take a fuckin' shot at me and then try to put me in a frame for assaulting Alex Benson."

He finally surrendered to the impulse and opened another beer, this time without offering one to me. Shaking his head, he said, "You really don't get it, do you Jack?"

Waving his arm in the direction of the fields around us, he said, "When you get right down to it, Cousin, all of this came down to me because my fuckin' grandfather stole that money from the bank. If he hadn't, maybe he would have gone belly up. My father wouldn't have taken over this farm, and I wouldn't have had to do it either. I could have done something entirely different with my life. But no matter, Jack, this *is* my life. I can't help how it came down to me, but since it has, I damned well need to protect it.

"You've already learned that there are still people around here who are pissed about the fact that that goddamned bank failed, taking at least some of their family's money with it. What do you think those assholes are going to do when they discover that their money has been sitting right in front of them all these years out there in these fields?

"I doubt very much that the sheriff can make a case for murder against my grandfather at this late date, no matter how much 'evidence' you think you've dug up. I don't think he can prove that either my grandfather or George Benson stole that money—at least he couldn't in a criminal case. But once you go down that road, people will be crawling out of the woodwork, filing civil suits against me, insisting that this farm was bought with money stolen from their ancestors and that they want it back."

He took a long drink of the Stella and looked over to me. "I'm sorry, but I can't let that happen. My whole life is in this farm. I'm fifty-six fuckin' years old, and I can't lose everything now."

"So, what do you propose to do about it?"

He set down his beer and reached into a tan canvass bag that was sitting on the other side of his chair. His hand came out of the bag closed around what appeared to be a .38 caliber revolver. I shook my head and said, "Oh, come the fuck on, Bud. Your grandfather killed my grandfather to cover up the crime he committed and now you think you're going to kill me to keep it covered up?"

"Sorry, but as I said, I really don't have a choice."

"Of course you do, and for what it's worth, killing me is not really going to make any difference. Late this afternoon, when I realized what had actually happened, I left a copy of my research notes in a very safe place. If I don't show up to get them later tonight, they'll go to the sheriff first thing in the morning and this will all be public anyhow."

He laughed. "Bullshit, Jack. People are always making threats like that in the movies and on TV shows when they're trying to save their goddamned skin, but they've never really actually done it."

"This isn't the movies, and believe me, I really did do it."

"I don't believe you and either way, it really doesn't make a difference."

"Tell me one more thing, then. When you wrote the note that you left at the library, were you careful about getting fingerprints on the paper when you took it out of the printer and put it in the envelope? I ask because the sheriff sent the note off to the crime lab over in Pierre, and if they raise your prints from it and then something happens to me, he'll be on your doorstep first thing."

"Don't worry about that. He's not going to find any of my fingerprints on the letter or on the envelope. And I sealed it with tap water, so he won't be getting any DNA from the envelope either."

Still pointing the gun at me, he stood up from the chair, wobbling a bit, perhaps as a result of all the beer he'd consumed. He took a step back and said, "You need to stand up now, Jack."

33.

I stood slowly and backed a couple of steps away from him. Throughout our conversation, the dog, Cody, had remained lying on the floor of the porch between us. Continuing to lie there, he now began moving his head back and forth, looking from me to Bud and back again, as if trying to divine what might be going on.

Waving the gun in the direction of the stairs, my cousin said, "Let's head on over to the barn."

Backing slowly down the stairs, I said, "Tell me Bud, have you ever actually shot anyone? Believe me, it's not as easy as it looks on TV."

"I guess I'll break my cherry on you, Cousin, unless you do exactly what I tell you to do."

"You know, I'm really beginning to regret the fact that Meg introduced us in the café the other day."

"Very funny. Now walk over to the fuckin' barn and open the door."

I had no idea what in the hell my cousin intended to do once we got out to the barn, and I really wasn't kidding when I told him that it's not all that easy to look another person in the eye and shoot him. But then maybe he really didn't intend to shoot me. Perhaps he intended to arrange some sort of tragic fatal "accident" out in the barn. Or maybe I would commit "suicide," like my poor grandfather.

I knew that he'd had at least five beers over a fairly short span of time. I wondered if he'd been trying to build up his courage, but I was also hoping that the alcohol might muddy his thinking and slow his reaction time at least a little. We reached the barn and I pulled the door open. Standing aside, I said, "After you, Cousin."

He smiled and shook his head. "You go first. The light switch is on the wall to your right."

I walked through the door, found the switch, and turned it on. The barn was suddenly awash in light and looking up I saw a bank of fixtures hanging in a row from the building's high ceiling. The place appeared to be more of a maintenance building rather than an actual barn. There were no animals in residence and no stalls in which any animals might have resided.

The building had a concrete floor, and a couple of tractors and a few other pieces of agricultural equipment were parked inside, along with a large Toyota pickup truck and a couple of ATVs. Two long work benches held a variety of tools, and it appeared that this was where my cousin stored and serviced his equipment. Using the gun, Bud waved me over in the direction of the ATVs. "Ever ridden an all-terrain vehicle, Jack?"

"No. Can't say as I ever have."

"Well, there's a first time for everything, and it's really not all that hard to learn."

Turning to him, I said, "You know, Bud, I don't think I really want to learn. I'm not in the mood to go for a ride."

"You seem to be forgetting that I'm the guy with the gun here. Now walk over there and climb into the seat of the green ATV."

The two ATVs were lined up, one behind the other, facing a small garage door. A tow bar connected the two machines so that one could pull the other, and on the rear machine—the green one—a link of heavy chain had been secured to a hitch behind the seat. The chain was then draped up and over the seat.

I stopped beside the machine and my cousin again waved his pistol. "Up into the seat now, Jack. Then once you're settled in, wrap that chain around your waist and secure it with the open paddle lock that's sitting on the dash."

I was now pretty sure that I knew what his plan was. Once I was trapped in the seat, he would probably smash me in the head with a hammer or some such thing. Then, once it got dark, he'd tow my machine out down the road and tip it over somewhere. Then he'd race back to the house, call the sheriff's office in a panic, and tell them that there had been a terrible accident.

He'd explain that we'd had a few beers and that I'd insisted that he give me a chance to ride one of his ATVs. We'd gone tearing off down the road together and I'd somehow managed to flip my machine and had been thrown off, hitting my head on a rock. He'd never forgive himself for allowing me to ride the machine in that condition.

I didn't much like the scenario, but as he had pointed out, he was the man with the gun. I climbed up into the seat as directed and wrapped the chain around my waist. "Pull it tight now, Cuz," he insisted.

I pulled the chain fairly tight then reached out for the paddle lock and fumbled it, dropping it onto the floor of the ATV near my left foot. "Oh shit," I said, "I'm a little nervous here, sorry."

I reached over as if to pick up the lock and pulled the pistol from my ankle holster. Then I turned and shot my cousin high in the right thigh.

* * *

Bud fell to the floor, dropping his gun in the process. I ran over, kicked it away from him and knelt down beside him. "Oh fuck, you shot me."

"Sorry about that, but I really didn't like the alternative program that you had mapped out."

"Oh Christ, that hurts. I'm dying, Jack."

"No, you're not. At least not if you do exactly what I say. Now lie still, shut the hell up, and don't go into shock on me."

I pulled the belt out of my jeans, wrapped it around his thigh just above the wound and cinched it down tight. Bud was

214

perspiring heavily and, in spite of my warning, he was clearly going into shock. I patted his arm and said, "Hang in there Cuz."

Then I pulled out my phone, punched in 9-1-1, and told the dispatcher that we needed an ambulance and the sheriff out at the Daniels Farm, ASAP.

34.

Probably needless to say, I did not get out of Tyndall as scheduled the following day. The ambulance appeared practically within minutes of my call and whisked my cousin off to the hospital. He'd spend several days there and would require major surgery, but the wound was not life-threatening.

I spent several long hours over that night and the next day, sitting with Sheriff Davis and the County Prosecutor, explaining the actions I'd taken and laying out the evidence that I'd found. In the end, they agreed that I had acted in self-defense and that there would be no charges filed against me for shooting Bud Daniels. Figuring that he'd suffered enough and that he was bound to suffer even more as the news leaked out, I refused to sign any charges against him for taking a shot at me and for then attempting to abduct me at gunpoint.

Over the next several weeks, the sheriff's office and the county attorney would mount a new investigation into the events that had occurred surrounding the demise of the Security Bank in the spring of 1925, and they would ultimately issue a statement absolving my grandfather of any blame for the embezzlements that had led to the bank's failure. The report also concluded that he had not taken his own life but rather that he had almost certainly been murdered by another party.

As I knew would be the case, the evidence at this point was not strong enough for the sheriff and the County Attorney to state with certainty that Joseph Daniels had killed my grandfather or that he and/or George Benson had stolen the money from the bank. Their statement basically waltzed around the subject, but in several very prominent stories, the area newspapers laid out the facts of the situation in such a way that people didn't have to read very closely between the lines to realize what had almost certainly happened. The wire services and the cable news people also jumped on the story, touting the fact that, after nearly a century, some level of justice had finally been served in the case.

Meanwhile, on a misty Monday morning, I finally checked out of the Welcome Inn Motel and pointed the Chrysler in the direction of the Czech National Cemetery. At my grandparents' graves I laid a bright red rose across each of their markers, then I stood there in the light rain, thinking about their lives and about the events that had brought me to this moment.

Finally, after several minutes, I leaned over, touched a hand to each of their headstones, and said a final, silent goodbye. Then I rose to my feet and took the first few steps that would lead me back home to Phoenix and to Annie.

The Security Bank of Tyndall

Author's Note

Once, when I was a very young boy, I asked my mother how my grandfather—her father—had died. She told me that he'd been killed in a bank robbery and then she quickly changed the subject and never mentioned his name again.

This book is based very loosely, then, on the events surrounding the death of my grandfather, Charles L. Bohac, who took his own life on Wednesday, May 20, 1925, in the vault of the Security Bank of Tyndall, South Dakota where he was employed as the assistant cashier. Born in Crete, Nebraska in 1877, he attended the public schools there. He then attended Doane College and the Omaha Business College. He moved to Tyndall in 1902 to join the family of his eldest sister, Mary, who was married to Joseph Zitka, the Bon Homme County Treasurer.

Zitka hired my grandfather to be the Assistant County Treasurer, and my grandfather was later elected County Treasurer himself. He also worked at the Security Bank in Tyndall and then at another bank in Scotland, South Dakota. During his years in Tyndall, he was a member of the Volunteer Fire Department, and on February 2, 1909, he married Anna Oliva. They would ultimately have four children, including my mother, Marie, who was born in Tyndall in June of 1919. In 1917, my grandfather returned to work as the assistant cashier at the Security Bank of Tyndall. At the time of his death, he was also serving as the Tyndall city auditor.

Prior to 1925, the Security Bank of Tyndall had existed for nearly fifty years and had survived several national economic downturns, including the catastrophic depression that began with the financial panic of 1893. In April of 1921, however, the bank's directors hired George E. Pfeifle as the institution's new cashier. Pfeifle was then twenty-eight years old, married with one adopted child. Prosecutors would later describe him as a man with a "good education" who came from "a respectable family."

Hiring Pfeifle, however, would prove to be the bank's undoing. He was an ambitious young man who was anxious to buy stock in the bank, and apparently his aim was to gain controlling interest of the institution. His only problem was that he had no money. Enter Frank Beddow, also a young man, who had already begun a life of crime and who had earlier been responsible for the failure of the Citizen's State Bank in Parker, South Dakota.

Acting together, Pfeifle and Beddow conspired to defraud the Security Bank in two ways. First, they implemented a check-kiting scheme that would ultimately cost the bank $48,000. Secondly, they conspired to steal certificates of deposit from the bank and cash them for their own profit.

At the time, the bank had several books of CDs. Pfeifle stole the last book in the series, one that he assumed (or hoped) would not be missed for some time. He took the book home with him and filled out several of the certificates in amounts ranging from $2500 to $10,000. He then gave the certificates to Beddow.

Beddow told Pfeifle that he would cash the CDs out of state and use the proceeds to buy land in California and Mexico. He convinced Pfeifle that he could then resell the lands fairly quickly at what he promised would be a significant profit. The money from the CDs could then be returned to the bank before the CDs were missed, and Pfeifle's share of the proceeds would be enough to purchase the shares in the bank that he coveted. A judge would later describe the scheme as "childlike," and commented that "how any person of mature mind could be led into such a scheme was beyond his understanding."

Sometime during the spring of 1925, my grandfather, the bank's assistant cashier, discovered at least a part of the scheme—

220

that relating to the check-kiting fraud. It's unclear if he realized the extent of the check-kiting scheme, and it's also unclear whether he ever realized that Pfeifle had also stolen the CDs. Whatever the case, for reasons only he could have explained, instead of immediately reporting his discovery to the bank's president or to the Board of Directors, my grandfather confronted Pfeifle about the bad checks. Pfeifle promised my grandfather that he would make good on the checks shortly and begged my him to give him a little time. My grandfather agreed to do so.

For a while, then, through April of 1925, the condition of the bank continued to appear sound, at least on the surface. On April 16, 1925, apparently as required by state banking regulations, the Security Bank published a "Statement of the Condition" of the bank in the *Tyndall Register*. According to the report prepared by Pfeifle in his capacity as cashier, the bank was in fine shape, and Pfeifle solemnly swore before a notary that "the above statement is true to the best of my knowledge and belief."

On May 14, 1925, The *Register* published the "Semi-Annual Report of C. L. Bohac, City Auditor," for the period ending March 31, 1925. The city's finances appeared to be in fine shape as well. In that same edition, the paper published a notice of a special city election also signed by my grandfather as the City Auditor.

Charles L. Bohac (standing) and George E. Pfeifle
in the Security Bank of Tyndall, circa 1924

Shortly thereafter, however "irregularities" were discovered in
the bank's accounts, and in the middle of May, members of the
bank's Board of Directors were summoned to Sioux Falls, South
Dakota to meet with state banking regulators. There they learned
that the bank was short the $48,000 lost to the check-kiting fraud.

The officials returned to Tyndall and held an emergency meeting of the directors on Sunday, May 17. At that time, Pfeifle was fired and a new cashier, F. F. Chladek, was appointed. Three of the bank's directors offered up $48,000 of their own money to make good the shortage and to keep the bank on a sound financial footing.

Peter Byrne, the bank's president, then wrote an open letter to the public and to the bank's depositors, alerting them to the fact that there were problems at the bank, "due to bad management on the part of its recent cashier, George E. Pfeifle. Certain checks were cashed by him, which were later found to be spurious and probably worthless, and it is now doubtful whether anything can be realized on them."

Byrne expressed the hope that "the confidence of the public, which the institution enjoyed for nearly half a century, will not be shaken by this one incident. The loss has been entirely absorbed, the offender discharged, and a tried man placed in charge of the institution, and the management conscientiously believes that the bank is as strong and safe as any time in its history."

On Monday, May 18, Pfeifle was arrested and charged with making a false statement to the state bank examiners (the statement published on April 16). Bond was set at $5,000, which Pfeifle posted immediately. He was then arrested on additional charges of embezzlement and his bond was raised to $10,000. He was unable to raise the additional $5,000 and remained in jail.

On Tuesday, May 19, the bank's officers met with my grandfather, and at that time, he apparently confessed to the fact that he had known about the shortages and had not immediately reported them to the bank's officers. One can only imagine how contentious that meeting must have been. By that time, over one hundred and seventy-five banks had already failed in South Dakota due to the agricultural depression of the early Twenties, and the directors must have realized how very vulnerable their own bank could be as a result of the crisis that had been created by Pfeifle's thefts.

At that meeting, the directors "sharply criticized" my grandfather for failing to report the thefts, although they did not fire him. Bank officials and others would later speculate that he had "brooded over the fact" that he might be blamed, at least in part, for the bank's difficulties, but we can never know with any certainty what his state of mind must have been through the rest of that day and evening. He had been a prominent member of the community up to that point, and doubtless, he must have been very embarrassed and perhaps worried about what this disclosure would do to his standing in the community. Certainly, he must have been severely depressed.

On the morning of Wednesday, May 20, witnesses reported seeing my grandfather walking to work shortly after seven o'clock, which was apparently normal, but said that he was "walking much faster" than he usually did and "appeared to be in a hurry." Shortly after arriving at the bank, he went into the vault, and there he took his own life, using a shotgun belonging to the bank. The newly appointed cashier, F. F. Chladek, then arrived at the bank and saw a light on in the vault. Assuming that my grandfather was in the vault, he walked over to ask him a question and discovered the body.

The coroner was called, and my grandfather's body was removed to the local funeral home. Grandpa had left a note addressed to the bank's president, which read, "Mr. Byrne: I am innocent of any wrong. I see now that I should have told sooner but Geo. kept insisting every day that he would take up the checks. Please help my poor family as they are destitute, and God bless them all. How I love them. Charles."

The *Tyndall Register* reported his death the following day, noting that, "Mr. Bohac has been a trusted employee for a number of years and held the position of assistant cashier.... It is apparent that Mr. Bohac brooded over the fact that he might be blamed to a certain extent for the shortage, but officials of the bank do not think he is to blame in any way.... The deceased leaves a wife and four children who have the sympathy of the entire community."

My grandfather's funeral service was held at the family home on Friday, May 22. J. A. Dvorak, of Tabor, conducted the services, and the *Tyndall Register* reported that he gave "a very interesting and sympathetic talk, telling of the work of the deceased. A big crowd attended the funeral and paid their last respects to the deceased.... The firemen of which the deceased was a member attended in a body in uniforms and marched to the cemetery northeast of town. The *Register* joins the many, many friends in expressing sympathy to the bereaved family."

In addition to the *Register* and the *Tribune*, a number of regional newspapers reported my grandfather's suicide and the problems afflicting the Security Bank. Shortly after my grandfather's death, reports surfaced linking Pfeifle to Frank Beddow. In an article datelined Tyndall, May 22, 1925, the *Rapid City Journal* reported that "Frank Beddows [sic.] of Sioux City, Ia., and his lieutenant are believed to be mixed up in the conditions which caused Charles Bohac, assistant cashier of the Security Bank of Tyndall, to commit suicide yesterday morning in the bank vault.

"George Pfeifle, assistant cashier, cashed worthless checks for Beddow and others believed to be his confederates to the amount of more than $40,000. Guaranty of the losses has been made by the directors of the bank and the bank is in operation today as usual."

"'We have as yet nothing to substantiate the Beddows [sic.]-Pfeifle connection but it seems almost certain that the two men were working together to defraud and wreck the bank,' the cashier [F. F. Chladek] stated."

In that, they were successful. The second element of the fraud involving the stolen certificates of deposit, was now uncovered. Initially, no one knew how many of the certificates might be in circulation or what value they might have, and it was feared that Pfeifle might have given Beddow fraudulent CDs worth as much as $500,000. Ultimately it turned out that the amount was a little over $145,000, which, combined with the money lost in the check-kiting scheme, put the bank's losses to Pfeifle and Beddow at nearly $200,000. State regulators determined that the bank could not survive a loss of that magnitude and on June 1, the Security Bank was closed and placed in the hands of state banking officials.

The initial hope was that the bank could quickly be reorganized as the Bank of Tyndall, and a plan was devised under which, over a period of three years, the new bank would make good the losses of those who had trusted their money to the Security Bank. However, state banking officials ultimately refused to grant a charter to the proposed new bank.

The principal sticking point involved the fraudulent certificates of deposit. State banking officials immediately ruled that the CDs had been issued spuriously and would not be honored as liabilities against the bank. They realized, however, that many of the CDs in question had been acquired by innocent victims of Beddow's scheme and that these people had no way of knowing that the CDs in their possession were not legitimate. Banking officials realized that these people would sue, and that the ultimate decision would rest with the courts. This would take many months and until the issue was settled it would be impossible to know what the true financial position of the Security Bank actually was.

When the effort to organize a new bank failed, state banking officials began the process of liquidating the affairs of the Security Bank so that its depositors and other creditors could get back as much of the money they had entrusted to the bank as possible.

This process would play out over the next several years and would not go well for the people of Bon Homme County.

Virtually all the assets of the bank were tied up in the mortgage and other loans that the bank had made. Theoretically, those who had borrowed money from the bank would repay their debts and state bank officials would then use those proceeds to repay the bank's depositors. Sadly, though, at a time when farm prices were bottoming out and land values were falling rapidly, many farmers who had borrowed money from the bank simply weren't able to repay their loans. State banking officials were then forced to foreclose on the lands and sell off the properties for whatever they could get in a depressed market.

In addition to the private citizens who had entrusted their money to the Security Bank, the failure of the bank had serious consequences for the Tyndall city government and for the Bon Homme County government as well. On July 27, the *Sioux City Journal* reported that "A report made by the county treasurer shows Bon Homme county has $90,740 tied up in closed banks. Of this amount $39,696 is in the failed Security Bank of Tyndall." The town of Tyndall had entrusted approximately $22,000 to the bank.

Meanwhile, an arrest warrant was issued for Frank Beddow who had gone on the run and who was rumored to be in Chicago, or perhaps in Argentina. On July 14, 1925, The *Des Moines Tribune* reported that "Beddow's expensively furnished office in Sioux City has been closed. The furniture has disappeared as has his fleet of automobiles, A lien for more than $100,000 unpaid income tax was recently filed against Beddow by the internal revenue collector for Iowa."

In mid-August 1925, George Pfeifle negotiated a plea deal with prosecutors and pled guilty to a charge of making false reports to state banking regulators. He was sentenced to two and a half years in the state penitentiary and was credited with the time he had already served in the Bon Homme County Jail. As a condition of the agreement, Pfeifle agreed to "reveal anything and everything pertaining to his dealings as cashier of the Security Bank of Tyndall, and particularly to his dealings with Frank R. Beddow."

On August 15, 1925, Pfeifle testified under oath regarding all his dealings and transactions with Beddow. The *Tyndall Tribune* reported that during the meeting, "Pfeifle was asked whether anyone in the city of Tyndall or immediate vicinity was connected with him, or in any way participated or assisted in the cashing of worthless checks and the issuance of spurious certificates of deposit. He answered that there were none, with the exception of endorsers of checks which were afterwards found to be worthless."

The *Tribune* reported that two other charges alleging embezzlement were still pending against Pfeifle. According to States Attorney William F. Hansen, "These charges will be held against him as a whip to compel him to testify in behalf of the state in any other criminal actions which may arise out of the failure of the Security Bank of Tyndall, and particularly against Frank Beddow whose connections with the bank deal, it is alleged, are such as will warrant criminal prosecution in the event Beddow can be apprehended. According to rumor, Beddow is at the present time in Argentina, South America."

Late in October 1925, state banking regulators rejected claims of $111,600 against the Security Bank in what the regulators described as "spurious" certificates of deposit. Claimants were given three months to take legal action in support of their claims, otherwise the regulators' decision would be deemed final. On October 22, the *Tyndall Tribune* reported that "Whether or not the claims of the spurious certificates of deposit can be collected is a matter for the courts to decide, but it is thought that in all of the cases where claims have been filed that action will be brought to try and recover on them. The state banking department will resist any action brought on the above claims, and payment will not be made unless the court so decrees."

At the end of January, Frank Beddow was finally arrested in Long Beach, California, where he had been working as a salesman under the alias of John Mooney. On January 30, 1926, the *Minneapolis Star* reported that Beddow was "under indictment in Tyndall, S.D., on a charge of using the mails to defraud. According to the Post Office Inspector, W. J. Maries of St. Paul, Minn., Beddow came to Los Angeles, deserting his family, and secret indictments were returned against him in December. Five other defendants were indicted with Beddow. These include George E. Pfeifle, formerly cashier of the Security Bank of Tyndall."

Finally, in February 1926, a full eight months after the Security Bank had failed, state banking officials sent out checks to creditors of the bank for ten percent of the money they had lost due to the failure of the bank. The total payout amount to a little over $60,000. The creditors also received interest-bearing certificates for the other ninety percent of the money they were owed. These certificates were negotiable and could be transferred.

On March 4, 1926, the *Tyndall Register* published an open letter from F. F. Chladek on the "Condition of the Security Bank." Chladek noted that banking officials were working diligently to liquidate the affairs of the bank and make payments to the bank's depositors, and that "It is the plan of the Examiner in Charge and the Department of Banking to pay dividends to the depositors whenever sufficient funds are on hand to pay a ten percent dividend."

Chladek further noted that the ability of officials to reimburse the bank's depositors was wholly dependent on the ability and the willingness of those who had borrowed money from the bank repaying their loans: "A good crop during the coming year and good prices for the crop will make a tremendous difference in the amount of liquidation to be secured in this bank."

In the meantime, Frank Beddow was extradited from California and set to stand trial in federal court in Sioux Falls on April 6, 1926. Before the trial could begin, however, Beddow and George Pfeifle pled guilty to charges of using the United States Mail to defraud. On April 10, 1926, the *Rapid City Journal* reported that Beddow was fined $6,000 and sentenced to five years in prison after pleading guilty to two charges. Pfeifle was sentenced to serve two years in the penitentiary, the term to start at the expiration of his existing term. All other counts and indictments against these two were dismissed.

With Beddow and Pfeifle now in prison, on August 12, 1926, the *Tyndall Tribune* reported that a second 10% dividend would be paid on August 23 or 24. "At present there is sufficient money on hand to pay a dividend of 20 percent instead of 10 percent, but it has to be withheld until a decision is rendered on the actions that [have been] brought against the bank to recover on alleged spurious certificates of deposit. The cases in connection with the certificates of deposit were tried several months ago, but the presiding judge took them under advisement and as yet has failed to render his decision. If the decision is in favor of the bank another dividend may be expected soon thereafter."

Seven months later, on March 27, 1927, the *Tribune* reported that, "SECURITY BANK LOSES IN COURT FIGHT; Alleged Spurious Certificates of Deposit Held Valid by Decision." The paper noted that, "Judge W. W. Knight has decided in favor of the holders of the alleged spurious certificates of deposit issued by the Security Bank. The cases in connection with these certificates involve approximately $110,000 and were tried last summer at Lake Andes before Judge Knight. Decision has been deferred until now."

In his ruling, the judge noted that "The certificates of deposit in question were issued by Pfeifle while acting as cashier of the defendant corporation. The transaction involved in each of these cases was one which the respective plaintiff had no reason to believe did not relate to the affairs of the bank."

Attorneys for the bank stated that they would carry the cases to the supreme court, "where they believe they have a good chance of winning, basing their judgment upon supreme court decisions in other states in similar actions."

In September 1927, officials announced a third payment of ten percent to the Security Bank's creditors. In the interim, the *Tyndall Register* had been sold and renamed the *Bon Homme County Register*. The paper reported that, "Creditors of the Security Bank received their checks this week under the third dividend declaration made by the state department recently. This payment distributes about $60,000 in this community, which ought to help financial conditions and increase the amount of exchange in business channels."

In August 1928, banking officials made a fourth payment of ten percent to the bank's depositors. In that same month, Frank Beddow and George Pfeifle were paroled from prison after serving only a little more than two years of the sentences they had been given. The Sioux City *Argus-Leader* reported that, the prisoners were granted their parole because the parole board felt that they "would not be a menace to society if released."

While Pfeifle was incarcerated, his wife and child had continued to reside in Tyndall. On August 16, 1928, the *Tyndall Tribune* reported that Pfeifle had been released from prison and had returned to Tyndall the Wednesday evening following his release. The paper noted that, "it is not thought that he will make his home here."

Over the succeeding years, Pfeifle held a variety of jobs and ultimately became a landscape architect. On June 1, 1973, at the age of eighty, he died following a traffic accident in Rock Island, Illinois. Police reported that he failed to stop for a stop sign and was struck by another vehicle.

Frank Beddow, however, would return almost immediately to a life of crime. He continued to work one swindle after another and was repeatedly arrested and jailed. On one occasion in 1934, he broke out of jail but thirty hours later, he and his girlfriend were found hiding in a pile of hay and he was returned to jail. Into the middle 1950s, he was still in trouble with the law, and he finally died in Dubuque, Iowa in 1979 at the age of 82.

Meanwhile, on January 10, 1929, the *Tyndall Tribune* reported that the state supreme court had reversed the decision of the circuit court in the matter of the fraudulent certificates of deposit issued by George Pfeifle. The court's decision meant that the spurious certificates would not be considered obligations against the Security Bank.

A year later, in January 1930, creditors of the Security Bank received a fifth dividend payment of ten percent, meaning that nearly five years after the bank had failed, they had now received back fifty percent of the money owed them by the bank. By then, though, the nation-wide Great Depression was in full swing and further payments apparently became impossible. In October of 1932, the bank's creditors each received a dividend check of three-quarters of one percent of the money they were still owed, and that would apparently be the last return they would ever get from the Security Bank of Tyndall.

In a letter to the depositors and other creditors of the bank, the new State Superintendent of Banks, E. A. Rudin, noted that, "Eventually there may be a small final dividend paid, when certain other assets have been liquidated and converted to cash." If this ever happened, I found no record of it, and thus it would appear that those depositors and other creditors of the bank ultimately got back just a tiny fraction over fifty percent of the money they had lost in the Security Bank, paid out over a period of seven years.

As things continued to go from bad to worse, Tyndall's only other bank, the First National Bank, failed in July 1932, due to "depleted reserves and frozen assets." In better news, though, at the end of that year, a new bank, the Security State Bank, was organized in Tyndall. Initially, the bank operated out of the old Security Bank building but after a few years it moved down the street to its current location on Main Street where the First National Bank had been located. No doubt fortified by the banking reforms that were made during the New Deal and after, it has remained in operation continuously since the end of 1932.

Following my mother's death, my siblings and I inherited, among other things, a cardboard box filled with old photographs much like the one I described in this novel. And in the bottom of the box, just as I have described, was a postcard that my grandfather had sent to my mother in 1919 and a photo of him taken in 1909.

By a vote of my brothers and sisters, I was designated the Family Archivist and given charge of the photos. With the help of my mother's cousin, I identified as many of the people in the photos as I could and then catalogued and preserved them. Like my protagonist, Jack Oliva, I made a copy of my grandfather's photo and set it on a shelf in my study.

Unlike Jack, I'm sorry to say, it took me a good many years to begin unraveling the mystery surrounding my grandfather's death. But with the advent of the Internet and particularly with the founding of Ancestry.com, I began tracing my family's genealogy and ultimately produced a family tree and a brief chronology of the family's history.

At that time, there were very few historical newspapers available on the Internet and so one summer, while enroute to Montana from Illinois, I detoured through Tyndall to read copies of the Tyndall newspapers in the library there. It was only then, reading the Tyndall papers for May 1925, that I realized for the first time that my grandfather had taken his own life.

That evening, I had a couple of beers in a bar called the Sportsman's Rendezvous, which was then located in the former Security Bank building. The owner, Eric Tycz, told me the story of my grandfather's ghost allegedly haunting the building and showed me the picture of my grandfather and George Pfeifle that he had discovered and hung on the wall of the bar. He also showed me the space in the bar's kitchen where the vault had once stood and where my grandfather had died. So many years after I had innocently asked my mother what I thought was a relatively simple question, it was one of the most surreal afternoons of my life.

In the short amount of time I had on that visit, I was able to get only a very rough idea of the circumstances surrounding my grandfather's death, but I summed them up as best I could in the short history that I wrote for the members of my family. A few years later, my brother Pat then picked up the baton and spent a great deal of time following the actors in this drama, principally George Pfeifle and Frank Beddow, through the census reports and newspapers online through their trials and imprisonment and ultimately to their deaths. On reading the material that Pat put together, I was stunned to learn that Pfeifle, the man perhaps most responsible for the circumstances that led my grandfather's death, had spent the last years of his life in Rock Island, Illinois and that he had died there, within four or five miles of the home where I then lived in Illinois.

At some point later, one of my other siblings, my sister Teresa, I believe, suggested that there might be a novel in all of this, but for a long time I couldn't figure out a way into such a book. In addition, I was at the time hard at work on a series of novels featuring a Phoenix homicide detective named Sean Richardson and didn't have the time to think about a project like this. But then at the end of 2018, I wrote a Sean Richardson novel titled *South of the Deuce*. In the novel Richardson investigates a series of contemporary murders that echo back to an unsolved series of killings from the late 1970s.

In investigating the crimes, Richardson contacts Jack Oliva, the lead detective in the original cases. Oliva briefly comes out of retirement to assist Richardson and then fades back into retirement once the case is over. But after finishing that book it occurred to me that Jack Oliva would be the ideal detective to investigate the circumstances surrounding my grandfather's death. There may have been something subconscious in play here from the very beginning since, when I was trying to come up with the name for the character in *South of the Deuce*, I gave him my grandmother's maiden name. And thus, the idea for this book was born.

Several years earlier, I had learned that my grandmother had told a variation of the bank robbery story to my cousin Sally. When Sally had asked how our grandfather had died, Grandma told her that he had discovered a fraud in the bank (so far, so good), and that the bank president had conspired with the local sheriff to murder my grandfather to cover up the fraud. (Clearly, my grandma had a pretty good imagination herself.) But thinking about that story was obviously important to the plot of the book, and so I'm indebted to Grandma for that and, in consequence, I have forgiven her for the Jim Beam episode, which actually did occur when I was five or six years old.

Finally having an idea for the story, I returned to Tyndall in the summer of 2019, and, like Jack, spent some time reading the Tyndall newspapers on microfilm in the library. (As yet they are not available on the Internet.) I spent a very pleasant few days exploring the town and got a chance to visit the museum and the volunteer fire department, where my grandfather's picture still hangs on the wall in a collage from 1905. The department also still has, stored in a corner of the fire station, the hand-drawn water pump that my grandfather helped to pull through the streets of Tyndall as a volunteer firefighter.

At that time, I was also able to visit again the building that once housed the Security Bank of Tyndall. It is now vacant and has fallen into a serious state of disrepair, although I'm told that a new owner intends to renovate the building into a laundromat with some apartments. My grandfather's ghost may no longer be haunting the former bank, but his presence weighed very heavily upon me as I walked through the empty structure that morning.

I'm greatly indebted to my brother, Pat Thane, for the research he did on this topic. Thanks also to Joan Johnson at the Tyndall Public Library and to Bob Foley, Janet Wagner and Goldie Winckler at the Bon Homme Heritage Museum for the help that they so generously provided while I was working on this project in Tyndall.

Bob Wyffels provided much-needed assistance with respect to the agricultural activities that Jack observed in and around Tyndall, and Clyde Ewalt supplied information about the ways in which the farm implement business worked in the 1920s and '30s. As always, I'm grateful to Gene Robinson and the folks at Moonshine Cove for their efforts on this book.

Everything I know about guns I learned from my friend Joe Topel, and I sincerely appreciate his help. Any errors that might have crept in while Joe was explaining this material to me or while I was attempting to understand it are solely the responsibility of Anheuser-Busch.

I don't dare mention Joe's name here without also mentioning that of his brother Tom, who has been my friend since we were both five years old. Tom contributed nothing whatsoever to the writing of this book, but I sincerely enjoy the opportunity to have lunch with him on a regular basis while we discuss the fortunes and misfortunes of our two favorite football teams, The Montana Grizzlies and the Indianapolis Colts.

In closing, I confess that I have no idea what my mother and grandmother might have thought of this book, especially since they were both so obviously reluctant to talk about my grandfather and the circumstances surrounding his death. The process of researching and writing it, though, made me feel that I was, at long last, establishing some sort of connection, no matter how tenuous, with the grandfather I never had a chance to know. I can only hope that they would have appreciated that.

CPSIA information can be obtained
at www.ICGtesting.com
Printed in the USA
LVHW042003061121
702620LV00017B/143

9 781952 439094